THE SUMMER LOVE STRATEGY

THE SUMMER LOVE STRATEGY

BY RAY STOEVE

Amulet Books • New York

Cataloging-in-Publication Data has been applied for and may be obtained from the Library of Congress.

ISBN 978-1-4197-6496-7

Text © 2024 Ray Stoeve

Illustrations by Beatriz Ramo

Book design by Deena Micah Fleming

Printed and bound in U.S.A.

10 9 8 7 6 5 4 3 2 1

Amulet Books are available at special discounts when purchased in quantity for premiums and promotions as well as fundraising or educational use. Special editions can also be created to specification. For details, contact specialsales@abramsbooks.com or the address below.

Amulet Books® is a registered trademark of Harry N. Abrams, Inc.

ABRAMS The Art of Books
195 Broadway, New York, NY 10007
abramsbooks.com

For my friends. I love you.

CHAPTER ONE

I T'S THE FIRST day of summer and my heart is already broken.

"I'm never falling for a straight girl again," I say, flopping backward onto Talia's bed with a soft thump.

"I told you Sherika only liked boys," Talia says, rocking back and forth in her desk chair. I turn my head and glare at her. She shrugs, grinning, and rocks a bit faster. "Besides, you've liked queer girls before, too."

"I knooooowww." I drag my fingers down my face. "But they all have one thing in common. They don't know I exist." I roll over, smushing my face into the bed.

The chair stops squeaking, and Talia's weight settles beside me on the bed. "I'm sorry."

I let out a long groan into the mattress.

"Hayley."

"Talia."

"You're gonna find a girl who likes you back, I promise."

"Yeah, right." Her purple comforter is soft under my cheek.

"At least it's summer now so you don't have to see her and Trey together," she says.

"What if he comes to see her at our basketball practices?" I started an offseason practice group last year, and according to Mariah, my friend and our junior varsity point guard, Sherika's planning on joining us this summer.

"Maybe it'll help you get over her?" Talia pokes me.

With a huge sigh, I turn over to face her. Like me, her usually white skin is still a little sunburned from the outdoor games we did for our last gym class of the year. She's lying on her back, looking at the stars scattered across her ceiling. They're not glowing because it's the middle of the afternoon and a perfect sunny day, but I've spent so many sleepovers staring up at them that I've memorized all the constellations. Talia loved astronomy as a kid, and even though she's not into it so much anymore, she's kept all the stars up there. It's a comforting constant: her spacious room with its sky-blue walls and huge closet opposite the door, her bed positioned between the two windows on the left-hand wall so it takes up most of the floor space in between. On one side of it is her nightstand; on the other is her desk, built by her dad during his woodworking era. On the walls around us, posters of her favorite bands and a bulletin board covered in layers of photos and papers and other mementos. And above us, the stars.

"Hey, you cleaned your room." I didn't notice it when I got here, but I feel kind of silly for not saying something before. She almost never cleans her room—not that she needs to. Next to me, she looks like a neat freak.

"Mom made me," Talia says. "Said it would be a 'fresh start

for the new season.'" She air quotes the words and rolls her eyes. She's prickly today.

"Are you OK?"

She shrugs. "I just need to do my shot, but I'm out of estrogen."

"Is there a shortage again?" Talia is trans, and sometimes the estrogen she takes isn't available for some reason. I don't know why it's so hard to make the medicine people need, but apparently it happens pretty often. Whenever it does, Talia is stressed out for weeks.

"No, I just forgot to refill my prescription. It's OK, Mom's getting it today."

"That's good." I flop over onto my back again, and we both stare at the ceiling. That's the nice thing about being with Talia: we can talk or not, it doesn't really matter. The silence is as comfortable as our conversations.

I close my eyes, and the image flashes in my mind again: Sherika's post on social media this morning, the photo with Trey and the gushy caption. I'd noticed him hanging around her more often, but I didn't get that many glimpses of her during the day at school. She was a junior and I was a sophomore. I'd chosen to ignore the signs, I guess, hoping for something that now I know will never happen.

Just like every other crush.

The tears well up then and I sniffle, squeezing my eyes shut. I know it's stupid to cry over a girl who barely knows who I am, but I can't help it.

"Hey." Talia's weight shifts, and her hand curls around mine, squeezing it tight. I squeeze back. "I'm here."

"Thanks," I say, my voice watery. The ache in my chest eases just a little bit. I came over here as soon as I saw the post, and now I don't want to leave. Talia's room is so calming. "Hey, can I . . ."

"Spend the night?"

I laugh. "You read my mind."

"We could do an ice cream run, too."

"You're the best." I roll over, and we lie facing each other.

"I know." She grins at me. "Guess what else."

"What?"

"I saw that MUNA's touring this summer," she says. "And they're playing Seattle on a very special day."

"What?!" I sit up straight, looking down at her. "No way."

"Yup. They're going to be here on our birthday," she says, sitting up too. "I can get my parents to get us tickets. I bet there will be lots of cute queer girls there, too." She wiggles her eyebrows. "Maybe you'll meet someone who will make you forget about Sherika."

I can see it now. The stage. The lights, sweeping over us. The super-hot, super-cool members of MUNA rocking out as I lock eyes with a cutie. And Talia there to witness the historic moment.

Talia and I have always shared everything. We were born in the same hospital on the same day; we've gone to all the same schools; we came out to each other before we told anyone else;

and we were there for each other when I told my parents I am a lesbian and when she told her parents she is trans. She comes to all my basketball games, and I'm always down to hear about the latest book series she's obsessed with. We both love mint chocolate chip ice cream, and we're even the same height: five feet, nine inches. And since we were old enough to know what a birthday was, we've spent every single one together. There's no one I'd rather dance with to sad queer synth pop than Talia.

Maybe this won't be a completely terrible summer.

"Hayley!"

I swim up out of an awesome dream toward the sound of my name. I'm a little annoyed; in the dream I was kissing Sherika, and it was perfect. But that was a dream, and this is reality: I'm single, Sherika is dating Trey, and it's time for Sunday family brunch.

I spent the past few nights at Talia's, marathoning superhero movies—not our normal fare, but the thought of a romance movie made my heart hurt—and eating way too much ice cream. Just kidding; there's no such thing as too much ice cream. I do still like being in my own bed, so last night I came home to sleep. But Talia promised she'd come over today to check on me.

"Hayley! Pancakes are ready!" Sam pounds on my door and runs away down the hall. She's way too awake for a thirteen-year-old on a summer Sunday.

I groan and blink against the sunlight streaming into my room, then inch out of bed.

My room is a mess. Unlike Talia's mom, mine doesn't make me clean it. She was a punk in the eighties and nineties—and claims she still is—and therefore, she says she doesn't believe in trying to control children's personal space. My dad is the same way. It's not that we don't have rules; it's just that the rules make sense, and they let me and my sisters help decide them.

Besides, my room only looks like a mess to other people. I know where everything is.

The first thing I do when I get up is go to the window and breathe in deep. Summer always smells like flowers, and it helps that Mom and Dad planted a row of sweet-smelling bushes in the side yard below. Across from me, a hedge shields my room from the neighbor's house, but not from the morning sun. I painted my walls golden yellow, and the sun just adds to the warmth. Rainbow dots of light sparkle around the room from the faceted crystals hanging on my curtain rod. I got them when we went to the Fremont Sunday Market as a family last summer.

I dig through my pile of clean shirts and find the one I want, and then pull on my cutoffs. From the top of the stack of books beside my bedside table, I grab my phone from where it's been charging and swipe a brush through my hair with the other hand. Then I run downstairs to breakfast.

"Finally!" Sam says when I come in.

Everyone's already sitting around the table, waiting. Our dining room is right below my room, facing south, so sunlight comes in all day through the bank of windows, and the kitchen is beyond it. Bookshelves are built into the walls, filled with Mom and Dad's massive collection. In the center of the room is a hardwood table dappled with fingerpaint, cup rings, and scratches as evidence of the years of use we've gotten out of it. Our whole house is like this: comfortably cluttered, with aging, deep-cushioned thrift-store furniture, a different color accent wall in every room, cups forgotten on every surface. I love it.

Dad shakes his head and laughs. Mom's already dishing pancakes up, and my older sister, Ella, is texting furiously.

My dad says her name in that patient tone, and she sets the phone down. Our meals together are family time, so we're not supposed to have our phones out. I sit beside her. Then I do a double take across the table at Sam.

"Your hair!"

She pets her head, cheeks turning pink. Her shoulder-length green-streaked brown hair is gone, replaced by a skintight buzz.

"We did it this morning," Dad says, rubbing his palm over her scalp, and she grins.

"Can I touch?" I ask, and she leans forward. "Wow, it's so soft."

"Thanks," she says.

"Why . . . ?"

"I just felt like it," she says quickly in that Sam voice that means she's done talking about it. Sam's stubbornness is legendary in our family. If she doesn't want to do something, there's no way you can make her.

"Can we turn down the music?" Ella asks, and Mom does. She loves blasting punk and new wave while she and Dad cook on Sunday mornings, but Ella hates it. Well, she doesn't hate it, just how loud it is. Between the music and our family, something has to get turned down, and it's not going to be us.

"OK," Dad says, once we're all settled. "Weekly check-in time. What's the new news, what's the hot gossip? What's up, what's going down?"

"Oh my god," Ella mumbles. "You're so cringe."

He grins. "I'm fifty-two, I'm supposed to be cringe."

"That's one of the things I love about you," Mom says, and they kiss.

"Gross!" Sam says, making a face. Ella rolls her eyes. I just smile. Yeah, our parents are corny sometimes, but I kind of like it. I want to still be starry-eyed about my person when we're in our fifties.

"Carry on," Mom says, flapping her hand at us. "Answer the man."

"Well, there's this," Sam says, pointing at her head. She rubs it, staring down at her plate. "And . . . um . . . I don't want you to call me my full name anymore, for any reason ever. It's just Sam now, OK?" She says it really fast, looking at all of us like she's expecting a challenge.

We all nod and say some variant of "sure!" all at the same time. I'm pretty sure I know what's going on, but I don't want to rush her or make her self-conscious by pressing her on it.

"OK," she says and sits back. "You go, Ella."

"Um." Ella looks up, thinking. "I start my summer job tomorrow? And I'm feeling kind of, I don't know. Anxious, I guess."

"How come?" Mom asks.

Ella shrugs. "It's just a lot of new stuff to learn. And what if it's overwhelming or I'm not good at it?" One hand twirls her hair. She turned out a dark brunette, like Dad; my hair is starting to fade from its pastel-pink dye job, but it's usually blonde, like Mom (at least, when her hair isn't dyed punk-rock black). Sam is somewhere between the two of us.

"You love books, sweetie," Dad says. "You're gonna do fine."

Ella's going to college in the fall and got her first job this summer at a local bookstore. It makes sense; she fits the part. She's wearing a T-shirt with artwork of the *Pride and Prejudice* cover on it right now, and if it was winter, she'd probably have a cardigan from her massive collection on over it. Dad pats her arm. Her mouth twists, but she nods.

Then everyone looks at me. "Talia's coming over later," I say. "She's helping me through my heartbreak."

"I'm sorry about Sherika, honey," Mom says.

I pick at my pancake. "Thanks."

My family is probably used to this by now. I've had too many crushes to count, and when I like someone, I can't keep my mouth shut about them: how cute their smile is, whatever cool thing they wore today, how much I liked what they said in class. Well, except when it comes to telling the actual person I like.

"You'll find someone, sweetie," Dad says. "Probably when you least expect it."

"Totally," Mom says. She glances at Dad, smirking. "Maybe someone you usually avoid."

"Oh god." Ella buries her head in her hands. But I'm ready, leaning forward, hands clasped together. I love this story. I've heard it a million times and I never get tired of it.

"Like a flaky punk boy in a band?" Dad says, grinning at Mom.

"Well, you were a drummer. I was right to be cautious."

"Of course, of course."

"But then Debbie, my best friend at the time, set me up on a blind date." Mom laughs. "She told me to go to our favorite diner—"

"Beth's Café," Dad says.

"—at 7 P.M. So I put on my nicer battle jacket, not the one crusted with blood from that one show. You played that show, remember?"

Dad groans and shakes his head.

"And I walk in looking for this guy she's been talking up all week. And it's you. I almost walked out—"

"You'd dated way too many drummers!" I exclaim. I know this bit by heart.

Mom smiles at me. "Exactly."

"But I saw her before she could leave! I convinced her to stay for a milkshake, and we ended up hanging out there almost all night. They had to kick us off the arcade games eventually." Dad laughs.

"That's what I want," I say with a sigh, leaning back in my chair. "I want a story as cute as that."

"You'll get it. There's no rush." Mom digs into her scramble.

That's easy for her to say. She has her person. She doesn't have to worry about heartbreak or liking someone who has no idea she exists.

What if she's wrong? What if I never find someone?

I push the thought away and cut off another piece of pancake, letting the sweetness fill my mouth.

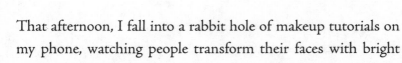

That afternoon, I fall into a rabbit hole of makeup tutorials on my phone, watching people transform their faces with bright eyeshadow looks. When someone clears their throat a few feet away from me, I shriek and bolt upright on my bed.

Talia grins at me. "Classic."

"Don't scare me like that! You *know* I'm dead to the world when I'm looking at a screen." I'm complaining, but I'm smiling, too.

"Hey, I was standing here for two whole minutes before I coughed the *slightest* of coughs to shake you out of your social media vortex."

"Whatever." I roll my eyes.

"Sam's hair looks cool."

"First of all, yes." I look at her. "But also, today she asked us—"

"Not to use her full name again ever? That was the first thing she said to me when she opened the door." Talia and Sam have a friendship of their own, almost like Talia had been Sam's babysitter growing up instead of my friend who's over at our house all the time. Sam always thought Talia was cool, but it really ramped up when Talia transitioned. At first, I thought all the questions Sam had for her were invasive, or offensive. But Talia had a different take.

"Do you think she's getting ready to come out as nonbinary?" Talia asks me now.

"I think so? It's been slow. She started dressing differently last year, more clothes from the boy's section, but mix and match, which is cool. And now the hair and name thing in one day. She was probably thinking about it for a while, though."

"Yeah, that's usually how it goes."

"I guess she'll do it when she's ready. If she is nonbinary. She might not be."

"Also true." Talia joins me on the bed. "What do you wanna do today? How are you feeling?"

I shrug. "I still feel shitty about the whole Sherika thing. Can we watch another movie? I think I'm ready for a romcom. I want to pretend that love isn't a lie."

"Oh my god, Hayley." Talia laughs. "OK. Let's distract you from your woes."

We scroll through the various streaming services on my laptop for way too long until we finally pick a movie, some office romance with an actress I kind of recognize, and settle back against the pillows. The opening credits roll, some cheesy pop song blasting through my Bluetooth speakers.

A few scenes in, the main characters have their meet-cute at a poolside cocktail party. One of them turns around from a conversation and runs right into the other one, knocking them into the water fully clothed.

"These movies make it look so easy," I say, watching the woman help the guy out of the pool in his soaking wet suit.

Talia nudges my arm. "Come on, you could do that."

"Knock someone into a pool?"

She laughs. "Well, yes. Knowing you, that's exactly what would happen."

I swat her arm. "Shut up!"

She rolls away from me, giggling. "I meant you could meet someone there."

"That's not a thing."

She rolls back. "You're just bummed because you're still pining for Sherika."

"No, I mean, that's not real life," I say, watching the movie but not really seeing it. "We go to the pool every summer, and nothing happens."

"OK, but we've never gone with the intention of meeting people," Talia says. "We could try."

"*We?*" I look over at her.

A small smile curls up the corners of her lips. "You know

how you have a new crush every month on people who never like you back?"

"Wow, you don't have to drag me like that."

"Oh my god, no, I just meant—" she shakes her head. "Like, that always happens to you, and I almost never like anyone. But what if we changed that this summer?"

"What do you mean?"

She pushes her tortoiseshell-frame glasses up on her nose. I can see the light in her eyes that she always gets when she's making a plan.

"Let's try and meet people. Like for real. Let's go to the pool and the concert and see if we can."

I raise my eyebrows, but it does have potential. Even if we don't find anyone, it could be fun. Besides, I need something to distract me from Sherika. My heart twinges at the thought of her: that gorgeous smile, her tall frame rising to block an opposing player, the bright colors she always wears that make her dark brown skin shine, how funny she is, and the way she always cheers the team on even when we're losing badly. We would have made such a good couple.

"OK," I say.

"Yes!" Talia pumps her fist.

I laugh. "You really want to do this? You want to find someone too?"

She shrugs. "I mean, that would be nice. And I get to help you feel better. Win-win."

I lean my head on her shoulder. The faint lavender smell of her lotion, shampoo, and conditioner—it's her favorite scent—drifts around me. Whether we really end up meeting girls this summer or not, it's fun to imagine trying and being each other's wingwomen, scoping out the hotties together. That sounds a lot better than pining for a girl I can't have.

CHAPTER TWO

W HEN I STEP inside the school gym for practice Monday morning, it's quiet. My shoes squeak as I cross to the closet where all the gear lives, and the sound echoes up into the high ceilings. The floor gleams, all the scuff marks gone, the outlines of the courts marked in our school colors: blue, green, and silver. The middle of the court is emblazoned with a stylized image of our mascot: the Salmon. It used to be an indigenous totem-style drawing a few years before I arrived, but all the school clubs for marginalized students, along with the social causes clubs and the white ally group, got together and petitioned for it to be changed because it was culturally appropriative.

I pause at center court, doing a slow turn to take everything in before the others arrive. The walls are decorated with championship victory flags across the years of Jefferson High School sports. The collapsible wooden bleachers are folded back against the wall, leaving full access to the three basketball courts stretching one beside the other. The six hoops sit silently across from each other, but I can almost hear the sound of our games: the basketball thumping off the backboard and swishing through the net or the clank when it misses and bounces off the rim instead, the shouts of girls calling for the pass or directing a teammate into position, the roar of the crowd when we make a basket. Not that the gym ever really roars for us; like a lot of schools, Jefferson High loves football first, boys' basketball second, and everything else is a distant third. We usually manage to get a small but respectable crowd of family and friends. But it's still annoying because we're good—like, *really* good.

As one of the taller girls on the JV team, I usually play power forward or shooting guard. When I'm power forward, my speed comes in handy, whether I'm shooting a three-pointer or zipping close to the basket to guard another player. I have to be bolder in that position, which I like. There's nothing better than going up against a bigger girl for a rebound and fighting the ball down into my arms instead of hers. When I'm shooting guard, I stay farther out from the hoop, closer to the point guard, taking passes and making long shots.

All those hours of shooting baskets in my driveway have paid off; I'm one of the best long-range shooters on JV. I've been playing since middle school: first at a local community center and then for the high school team. I was JV the past two years, but next year, I want to make varsity.

I open the gear closet and wheel out the crate of basketballs. From the back door that leads to the parking lot, I hear a thump.

"Hayley!" I'd know that loud, raspy voice anywhere. Mariah emerges onto the court, a big smile on her face. Trinity, the tallest and biggest girl on the JV team and our center, follows behind her, waving. They're both Black, like a lot of the girls on our team, but Mariah's skin is a lighter golden, and Trinity's is a deep dark brown. Mariah is friendly and assertive, which makes her a great fit for the leadership of point guard. Trinity is one of the quietest girls on the team, but she's rock-solid as center, fielding rebounds and getting in there to block even the most aggressive players.

"You ready for this? We making varsity next year, baby!" Mariah fist-bumps me, and Trinity smiles. They both drop their stuff by the bleachers, grab balls, and start warming up with me.

Anh, who's Vietnamese and our other point guard, arrives next, greeting us cheerfully, and the rest of the girls trickle in after her. I'm shooting baskets, running in for layups, but I'm tuned to the sound of that door opening and closing. Someone hooks their phone up to the sound system, blasting a playlist of viral hits to pump us up. The next time I glance back at the door, I see her.

Sherika.

She looks so good. She's one of a few varsity girls joining our meetup this summer. A lot of the other girls play club basketball when the school season is over, or go to fancy camps during the summer, but not all of us can afford that, so we do this instead. My family isn't low-income, but we don't have a lot of disposable money either, and it was Sam's turn to have a summer activity paid for this year. That's part of why Ella got a job, so she could pay for the fun things she wanted to do this summer.

This year, our practice group is smaller than usual, but so far, everyone seems as dedicated as me. We all agreed to meet

Monday through Friday, nine to noon, since some of the girls have jobs or other commitments the rest of the time.

"HAYLEY!" Mariah's voice echoes down the court, and I turn in time to catch the basketball flying toward my face.

I pivot and drive toward the basket, feet leaving the ground for a layup. *Swish.* Nothing but net. A perfect basket. I live for these moments—when everything syncs up and my brain goes quiet and I'm not everyday Hayley, zipping around school or home almost as fast as my racing thoughts; I'm basketball Hayley, part of a team, with nothing to worry about but the game.

"Nice one!" She jogs up for a high five. As our hands meet, her eyes drift over my shoulder. "Oh my god. Turn around."

I whirl around. *Did someone get injured already?*

Nope.

It's Sherika.

Walking toward me with a big smile on her face.

I feel like I just got struck by lightning, like I'm vibrating from the inside out. She lifts her hand, waving, and then suddenly she's right in front of me. She's a little taller than me, the perfect height to stretch up on my tiptoes and—

"So you're running this thing?" she asks.

"Yes! Yep. I am." *OK, Hayley, cool it with the affirmatives.* "I'm just the keyholder, actually, but I'm kind of in charge because of that." Keyholder is a big responsibility. It feels good that the girls—and Coach Kay—all trust me to set things up.

"Sweet. Do you want any help running drills?"

"That would be great!" I turn, scanning the gym. Looks like everyone's here. That buzzing feeling is still ricocheting through my body, but I'm entering basketball brain. "Let's see, we have twelve players today. I was thinking we could run lines to warm up, and then start on some shooting drills, end with some three-on-three, then hit the weight room. Maybe for the drills and the three-on-three, I could take five girls on the far court, and you take the other five to the other one? That way, we have an empty one in the middle so there's more space."

"Wow." She's nodding. "You should be a coach."

I wave my hand, blushing. "I just think about basketball a lot."

"I can see that." She cups her hands around her mouth and calls out, "OK, ladies, circle up!"

I turn to Mariah, and she widens her eyes at me. Mariah isn't queer, but sometimes I forget that. She's my go-to crush confidante on the team.

Oh my god, I mouth at her, then turn back toward the approaching girls. I'm fine. This is fine. Sherika and I just had our first significant interaction and EVERYTHING IS FINE.

When everyone is gathered around, I notice one of the varsity players has a hand raised. I point to her.

"Could we use a gender-neutral term instead of ladies? I'm nonbinary—they/them pronouns," they say.

"Oh, right!" Sherika smacks her forehead. "My bad, Jude. OK, let's do a quick name and pronoun round since we don't all know each other that well."

Of course she's a trans ally, too. And of course we finally start talking now, when I have to get over her.

I hope Trey knows how lucky he is.

On my way home from practice, I text Talia about the Sherika interaction.

I'm surprised you didn't faint on the spot, she says, with a smirky emoji.

I mean, same, I say. She's just sooooooo perfect. We would have been the cutest couple, smooching when she got to practice, playing varsity together, jumping into each other's arms after I pass her the ball and she sinks the game-winning point. She'd take me to Senior Prom with her and we'd be voted Prom Queens together—

My phone pings, jolting me out of my fantasy. She's just a person, Talia says. I'm sure she has flaws like anyone else.

I sigh. Trust Talia to bring me back down to earth. OK. Yes. You're right. Sherika's a well-rounded human. Trans allyship is the bare minimum.

I'd have to agree. Talia's humor is so dry it's practically a desert sometimes. I love it. Sometimes it's not even that she's trying to be funny, she's just being honest. But she's fine with me laughing, now that she knows I'm not laughing at her.

Really? I thought you hated trans people, I say.

Oh, absolutely I do. But even people I hate deserve rights.

I send a string of cry-laughing emojis. I'm not actually laughing that hard, but I'm definitely chuckling in my seat on the bus.

She sends a string of random emojis back, and then we're playing our game, where we make up a sentence to go with the emojis the other person just sent.

She sends me the levitating man, disco ball, and fire emoji; A mysterious stranger set the dance floor on fire, I write back, and send her the tulip, the donkey, the diamond ring, the scorpion, and a sunset.

Donkey and Scorpion's wedding was a magical sunset affair, she says.

What about the tulip?

It was a spring ceremony, she says. I snort.

It gets progressively weirder and weirder until I really am cackling. The person beside me shifts. I'm probably annoying everyone on the bus, but I don't care.

You should come over, she says finally. I got an idea.

Yeah? What?

You'll see!

Talia lives a ten-minute walk from me, so instead of taking the bus all the way home, I get off a few stops early and wind through the neighborhood. I could walk to her house in my sleep at this point. I climb the short set of steps up, and just as I reach her front porch, she opens the door.

"You're being very mysterious," I say as I walk up to her.

She shrugs, eyes gleaming. "Come into my lair."

I follow her inside. Her house is different from mine in almost every way. All the furniture is the same matching mid-century modern style, the walls are eggshell white, and there are big prints of beautiful landscapes hung in every room. There's a stack of half-read books on the end table by the couch and a coffee mug or two on the dining table, but everything is always neat and put away in its own spot. It's lived-in, like ours, but in a light and airy way.

We make our way to the back of the house where Talia's room is and flop onto her bed.

"I've been thinking," she says. "About the whole meeting-girls-this-summer thing."

I tilt my head and wait for her to continue.

"What if we did more than that? What if we made it a whole thing?" She sweeps her hands wide as if she's showing me something.

"What do you mean?"

"So, you know how romance movies always happen the same way? There's a cute spot where the love interests meet—like pools," she says, widening her eyes. "Concerts."

I watch her face. Her freckles are starting to come in, and they match her brown eyes.

"We could do that, too," she says.

"I thought that was the plan?" I'm not quite following her, even though she's smiling, rocking back and forth, stimming in excitement.

"Yes, but we could go *more* places." She shakes her hands vigorously as she says it. "We could do this systematically— come up with a strategy, with steps and goals and measurable progress markers."

"Huh. Like what?"

She gets up and digs through her bag until she pulls out a notebook and pen and comes back to the bed. On a fresh page, she draws three columns: one for DATE, one for PLACE, and one for GOALS. Her curly dark brown hair falls over her shoulders as she frowns, concentrating on drawing the lines. She looks up at me and smiles, her glasses halfway down her nose, her eyes sparkling. Knowing Talia, her brain has probably been whirring on this single track since she first came up with the idea.

"If you were going to try and meet girls around here, where would you go?" she asks.

"Well, it's supposed to be nice the second half of this week," I say slowly. "Maybe a beach? Like, on Lake Washington. Not Puget Sound."

"Way too cold," she agrees, shivering. "Then Pride is next weekend. That would be perfect because we're already going. And you have some teammates with summer birthdays, right?"

"Yeah! We have, like, three Cancers and three Leos on our team." That's not counting me, also a Cancer, and Talia. "So some of them will probably have—ohhhhh." We lock eyes. She's nodding. "Parties."

"Exactly," she says.

"You're a genius."

She flips her hair. "I know."

We grin at each other. I feel this sparkle rising inside me, like fireworks crackling. I get it now. The summer unfolds before me, hot and bright, us lounging on the beach, striding through Pride with perfect tans, eyes sparkling like the pool in the sun. On a double date with our new girlfriends, another thing we can do together, another memory we can share.

"We should do Magnuson Park for the beach," I say. "People have been tagging each other in posts there all month."

Talia writes it all down. "Then Pride. Then the pool, MUNA on our birthday, and wrap it up with a party. Boom." She mic-drops her pen.

"Which pool?" I stretch out on my stomach, looking at the different columns.

"Well, there's that outdoor one we went to last summer. But it's in West Seattle, so kind of far away." Talia wrinkles her nose.

"And none of us can drive."

"I know. Typical gays."

"So we'd have to get a ride from someone's parents. Or go to a closer one. We could ask Kev? His mom has some weekdays off."

Talia points at me and makes a note. We pick dates for each place and put big question marks next to the party. We'll have to wait on that one since no one's announced anything yet.

"OK. Now let's talk goals," Talia says.

"Finding love?" I grin at her.

"That's the macro goal," she says, writing it at the bottom of the columns. "But we need steps to get there. Like, what's our goal for each event? Practicing significant eye contact? Exchanging social media handles? Asking someone to go on a date?"

"Wow, you've really thought about this."

Talia shrugs. "Just autistic things."

I nod. Pretty much our whole group of friends is neurodivergent: Jacob and Talia are both autistic, and Bri thinks they might be, too. I'm not sure about myself, but I do know I have an anxiety disorder, diagnosed when I was in sixth grade. And Kev . . . Kev might be neurotypical, but he hangs out with us, so he's absorbed our mannerisms by default. I don't know about Bri's girlfriend, Karina, yet. She's only been dating Bri for a few months, so it's too soon to ask her such a personal question. At least, that's what I've learned from past mistakes.

So Talia's attention to detail here is no surprise. When she plans something, especially if it's something social, she *really* plans it. Social nuance doesn't come naturally to her, so she had to teach herself how to read people early on. It takes a lot of energy, though, and so does the general sensory overload of being out in the world, so she likes to space out big events.

"I guess I've never really thought about how to actually get a date," I say, rolling over onto my back and staring at the ceiling. "I always just got crushes and did nothing about them."

"At least you've had crushes," Talia says dryly. "I haven't had one since middle school." She lies down next to me.

I poke her. "There's nothing wrong with that."

She shrugs. "I guess."

I kick my feet in the air, thinking about the possibilities, listening to the birds outside.

"You wanna go wander around in Capitol Hill for a bit?" Talia asks.

"Yes, please!" I sit upright. My attention for strategizing was already starting to fade; Talia can always tell.

She heads to the bathroom while I wait. On the bed, the notebook lies open, and I glance at the page again. The breeze coming through the window carries the smell of the lilacs outside, and I close my eyes, breathing deeply. I can't help myself: I can see it now. This is how it all begins. This might be part of the story I tell later, about how I met my girlfriend.

Step one in the Summer Love Strategy: Magnuson Park on Thursday. Here's hoping the weather cooperates.

CHAPTER THREE

B Y TOMORROW AFTERNOON, though, the sun is gone, and Seattle's typical June haze descends with a cloudy, misty day in the high fifties.

"This is not the summer I was promised," Kevin grumbles, staring out the window of his room. Beside him, Jacob obliterates a zombie on the TV screen. Both of them are wearing the same *Stranger Things* T-shirt, which they insisted was an accident.

"You'd still be inside playing video games either way," Bri points out from the floor where they're drawing a new character in their sketchbook, their round face close to the page. From above, I have a perfect view of their short Afro dyed a fresh shade of teal.

"Yeah, but at least I'd get to look out at the sun instead of rain."

Bri snorts. I'm on Kev's bed, watching him and Jacob annihilating the undead for their latest livestream gaming session. Twenty more minutes of this and then we're meeting Talia and Karina for pizza.

"Who's that?" I ask Bri, pointing at the gray-skinned, muscled, ogre-like guy they've been working on. As I watch, they shade in the crossbow he's holding.

"My half-orc ranger," they say without looking up from their drawing. "He's my character for the new campaign we're playing."

Kevin, Jacob, and Bri are super into *Dungeons & Dragons*. Personally, I have no idea how they keep all the rules straight, let alone figure out their character stats, but whatever makes them happy. They're big-time nerds—or in Kev and Bri's case, Blerds, as they like to call themselves, short for Black nerds. Jacob's white, like me and Talia, but he gets a fun title, too: gaymer, since he's gay. When I was in middle school, I thought nerds were just the mean white boys who sat together trading *Magic: The Gathering* cards, but anyone can be a nerd.

Even though I'm not a nerd about video games and fantasy worlds, I'm nerdy about other things, like women's basketball and famous queer people. I can tell you exactly who's dating who right now in Hollywood, who just came out, and every rule of basketball down to the minutiae. I do think cosplay is fun, too, even though I don't know anything about most of the characters Bri asks me to dress up as for Halloween. But they all listen to me talk about Kristen Stewart, Janelle Monae, and who's going to the Olympics, and they come to all my games, so it's only fair I watch their livestreams.

I won't be mad when we're done, though.

A few minutes later, the prayers of my growling stomach are answered: Jacob sets down his controller and spins around as Kev logs them off. "You kids ready?"

"You're a kid, too," Bri says, unfolding their legs.

"We're sixteen," Jacob says, waving a hand loftily at himself and Kev. "The rest of you children are a mere fifteen."

"Shut up," I say, laughing. "Not for long."

He grins, placing his hands under his face like he's just an innocent angel, then runs ahead of us out of Kev's room. Bri chases him out.

"Aww, look at the little goblins go," Kev says, following them. He's easily the tallest of all of us, at six feet; Talia and I are next, and Bri and Jacob are the shorties of the group.

"I heard that!" Bri yells back from the foyer, and we both laugh.

We pile out the door and head down toward the International District. Our favorite shop, World Pizza, is a twenty-minute walk down from the Central District, where Kev lives with his parents and little brother. His older sibling, Parker, graduated before we started at Jefferson High School. They were part of the fight to get gender-neutral restrooms at the school, and now they're in college and home for the summer to get top surgery. They're technically Kev's stepsibling—Kev's dad met Parker's mom, who's white, on a dating site a few years after his biological mom died of cancer—but they've gotten pretty close over the years.

There's a bit of a breeze, but mostly it's just humid, and by the time we make it all the way down Jackson Street to World Pizza, I'm sweating. I tie my flannel around my waist, pulling my hair away from my neck into a ponytail. I worked so hard to get it this long, but I'm kind of over it now. Sometimes I want to cut it all off. Or dye it again, maybe lavender this time instead of pastel pink. Or both. Who says you can't have it all?

"Finally!" Karina calls from the booth at the back of the shop. "We've been waiting forever!"

"She means five minutes," Talia says, trying and failing to dodge as Karina pushes her shoulder.

We crowd up to the register, ordering a couple slices of pizza each, with soft drinks. The person behind the counter hands our orders out one by one and we all sit down, squishing in three to a side. I'm sandwiched between Talia and Kev, and Karina and Bri are right against each other on the other side, with Jacob on the aisle.

I've only known the rest of my friends since freshmen year, but sometimes it feels like I've known them just as long as Talia. We all fit together, and here in the booth with all of them I feel at home, like nothing can get to me. We stuff our faces, chattering about nothing and everything at once. The icy burn of root beer on my tongue wakes me up and cools me down. Bri snuggles under Karina's arm. Kevin uses my shoulder as an arm rest, and on my other side, Talia puts one leg over mine. We're all super comfortable with each other. Jacob doesn't touch anyone, but that's because he doesn't really like being touched. Bri and Karina try to give him as much space as possible, but eventually he gets up and grabs a chair from the front, pulling it up to the side of the table. Bri uses this as a chance to run to the bathroom, and Karina sprawls out across the whole bench, long legs sticking out into the aisle.

"So," she says, wiggling her eyebrows. "Who wants to get some Dick's this weekend?"

Kev snorts into his root beer. "Always."

The jokes about our favorite burger joint never stop being funny. Last summer, we ate there a few times a week at least. We'd go up to Capitol Hill, get our burgers, and go lie around in Cal Anderson Park, watching as it transformed into a combination sunset-date-night spot and neighborhood dog park.

"I love Dick's," Talia says, "but what if we did something different this summer?"

"Am I hearing right?" Bri asks, sliding back in beside Karina. "Talia wants to shake things up?"

"Shut up," Talia says, blushing. "I'm serious! Hayley and I . . ." she glances at me. "We have a plan."

"For world domination through spreadsheets and pop culture knowledge?" Jacob asks.

"Oh my god, let her finish." I roll my eyes.

And Talia tells them about our plan, laying out the sequence of events for the summer. Karina raises her eyebrows, but not in a skeptical way—more like she's curious. Bri's face stays neutral as always.

"That is so cute," Jacob says, hands clasped together. I know he's a huge romantic.

Kev nods slowly. "I like it."

"Talia even thought of all the smaller goals we need," I say, squeezing her arm. "Like getting people's info and practicing flirting and stuff."

"Do you know what you're looking for?" Jacob asks.

I tilt my head. "A girlfriend?"

He laughs. "No, like . . . what do you want in a girlfriend? Shared interests?"

"Hotness?" Kev interjects.

Karina takes a swipe at him from across the table. "A cool brain?" She smiles down at Bri, who breaks into a huge grin, pushing their face against her shoulder. Their relationship is so cute. It's so clear how much they like each other.

"We . . . didn't really think about that yet," Talia says.

"Maybe that could be your first task? Before the lake?" Jacob says. "Like, make a list of the qualities you're looking for. That way, it'll be easier to help each other find someone."

"That's a great idea." I look around at everyone. "So what do you think? Are you all in for the beach this Thursday?"

Everyone says yes except Karina, who's picking up a shift at her family's restaurant. They make some of the best Mexican food in Seattle, in my humble opinion.

"Talia, I've gotta give you credit for trying to shake Hayley out of her hopeless crush rut," Kevin says through his last mouthful of pizza. "I don't know how this is gonna work, but I definitely wanna be there to see it."

After we tell our friends about the plan, it seems more real. I think about Jacob's question the whole next day. It's in the back of my mind at practice while I watch Sherika sink perfect baskets; on the bus home while I stare out the window; during dinner while my sisters ramble on about their days. It should be easy to just sit down and make a list, but now that there's an actual task in front of me, I can't do it. This happens to me sometimes: I know I need to do a thing, but the more pressure there is, the more I avoid it.

Wednesday evening comes and the pressure builds all through dinner, and then it happens: that vibrating energy inside me, that I-have-to-do-this-NOW feeling like a faucet on full blast. Beach Day is tomorrow, and I'm out of time.

As soon as the plates are cleared from the table, I rush upstairs and dig through the pile of papers on my desk until I find an old school worksheet. The back is blank. Perfect.

I grab my favorite purple pen and clear a space on the desk, then sit down, staring at the blank page.

What do I want in a girlfriend?

Sherika is my most recent crush—thanks to our summer practice group, I know I'm not over her yet. I still feel that little ache in my chest when her face pops into my mind. What do I like about her? She's funny, encouraging, and, well, pretty. And her smile.

I don't know her that well, though. Before this group, I only had one real interaction, when she high-fived me after a practice.

My crush before that was Lindsay Holmes, who already had a girlfriend. She sat behind me in English and always needed to borrow a pen. I must have given her my entire pen collection over the course of the month. She was also really funny, but kind of mean to her friends. They were always so snarky with each other. But she had such long, beautiful red hair and these hazel eyes that just pinned me to my seat.

OK, so Sherika and Lindsay are both funny. I guess that's a data point, as Talia would say. On the paper, I write down the qualities I have so far: *funny, encouraging.* And both Lindsay and Sherika are really easy to be around. So I add that, too.

In middle school, I pretty much only hung out with Talia, so the girls I had crushes on didn't even know who I was. Some of them were really popular, and I'd imagine them sweeping me up in their glow. Some of them were more like me, quiet girls who had a close group of friends they hung out with. I pictured us talking for hours about our favorite movies and musicians.

That could be a quality: friendships are important to them. I write that down. But I don't want the pressure of being popular, of having to fit in. *Likes me for who I am,* I add. And *Fun to talk to.*

The list is short, and I feel weird about that. It's always been so easy to imagine having a girlfriend. It would be like Mom and Dad's story, only gay, and then we'd be cute and happy together for . . . well, maybe not the rest of our lives, but the future as far as I could see it. At least through senior year. I'm kind of fuzzy on what happens after that; it's far away, and I don't know yet where I want to go to college or what I want to do with my life. But I can imagine myself with a girlfriend at prom. I can picture the whole promposal, even, and us hanging out with my friends, and maybe her friends becoming friends with mine. But I never really thought about what I wanted beyond whoever I had a crush on in that moment. Even right now, in my head, this imaginary girlfriend still looks like Sherika.

I press the heel of my hand against my sternum, massaging it. My chest feels tight. I breathe in for four counts, hold it for four, then breathe out for the same count.

I remember when I first learned these breaths. It was in sixth grade, before I came out, and I had my first crush on a girl. Leia Matthews. Her parents were big *Star Wars* fans. I don't really like thinking about her, or that time in my life. She was straight, and I was closeted. I couldn't tell anyone I had a crush on her, but liking her and keeping it secret was making me so anxious I started having panic attacks at school. My whole body would fill with adrenaline, the classroom would fade away, and then I'd bolt and lock myself in the bathroom. My favorite teacher eventually found me there after class one day. Several meetings with the school counselor later, when I refused to say why I was freaking out, Mom took me to see a therapist. And the therapist taught me to do this breathing technique while I massage my sternum. Apparently, it helps you calm down. My therapist always talked a lot about nervous system regulation, but I didn't retain a whole lot of it.

"Hayley?"

I jump and look up. My mom is standing in the doorway.

"It's your night to do the dishes, honey," she says.

"Oh yeah!" I forgot about the dishes. I was too busy making the list. "Sorry."

She sighs, but she doesn't look mad, just amused. "I know you get sidetracked easily, so I just wanted to check in."

"Totally. I'll do them now."

She steps aside to let me pass. In the kitchen, I crank up some music and run hot water for the dishes in the sink. As the soap bubbles up, I space out, staring out the window at the hedge looming in the twilight.

I didn't expect making this list to be so hard. Is Talia having this much trouble? Knowing her, she probably knows exactly what she wants.

This was supposed to be fun. Both of us helping each other find dates. But now I'm kind of dreading tomorrow. I don't want to think about all these details. I just want to go to the lake and check out pretty girls.

I plunge a dish into the soapy water, my heart sinking along with it.

CHAPTER FOUR

I WAKE UP THE next morning with anxiety still thrumming in my chest. The sky outside is a perfect bright blue, the sun streams in, and my room smells like flowers—but all I can think about is that list. I have to catch the bus to practice and then head straight down to Magnuson Park afterward, which means I have to get moving now to get everything packed. So I drag myself out of bed, grab my phone, and blast some music to wake myself up.

Everyone is gone already, of course. Dad works for one of the local unions and Mom's a social worker, so they leave early. Sam is at art camp, and Ella has a shift at the bookstore. She came home yesterday buzzing with excitement. Thanks to her, I now know exactly how to ring up on a cash register.

I heat up a breakfast burrito and carry it back upstairs, eating with one hand while I rummage through my dresser with the other. Finally, in the last drawer (of course) I find my swimsuit wadded behind some pants.

I set the burrito down and hold up the suit. It's a cherry-red one piece with a halter top. I like it because it looks like something a pinup girl from the fifties would wear.

My body's definitely changed from last summer, though, because when I pull it on, it's way too tight. The pinch under my arms and around my thighs is very unpleasant. This isn't going to work at all.

So I do the logical thing: I raid Ella's closet. I know she hates it when people go in her room without asking, so I send her a text because I'm not a total jerk, but I don't have time to wait for her approval. Besides, it's not like I'm taking her new one. I find the one from last summer—the two-piece with the emerald-green high-waisted bottoms and the floral-print top that I always thought would look great on me—and it fits perfectly.

But as I pack my bag, my chest gets tighter and tighter, until I can't stand it anymore. Deep breathing isn't helping.

I head down to the bus and shoot Talia a text. Morning!! Beach Day!! Maybe I can fake it 'til I make it.

She texts back immediately. Cute girls here we come! You ready?

Oh god, she's totally excited about this. But I don't want to lie to her. Umm . . . yes and . . . I'm super anxious :(

OMG ME TOO

I laugh out loud, relief blooming in my chest. Do you still wanna do it?

Yes, totally. It's ok if we don't get anyone's info though.

Absolutely. I put my headphones in and pick my music for the ride, bobbing my head as the beat kicks in. I feel less anxious, but it still feels like a lot of pressure.

I text her again. You know how we talked about taking it in steps? Maybe today could be recon or something? Like just seeing who looks cute and stuff.

The ellipses pop up, showing me she's typing, and for a moment I feel so nervous I get nauseous. I don't want to disappoint her.

But I don't have to worry. This is Talia, and we have the same brain.

OMG, yes please, she says. Also the list is way harder than I thought it would be.

SAME, I say, adding a laughing emoji. The tightness in my chest eases up a little.

You're the best, Talia says, and I smile down at the screen.

No u, I say back, and slide the phone into my pocket. The lake shimmers in my mind, deep and cool under the hot sun. This is why I love Talia. We understand each other.

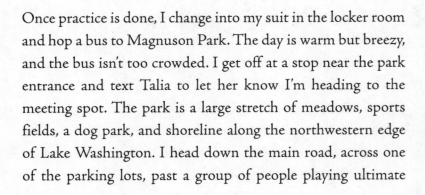

Once practice is done, I change into my suit in the locker room and hop a bus to Magnuson Park. The day is warm but breezy, and the bus isn't too crowded. I get off at a stop near the park entrance and text Talia to let her know I'm heading to the meeting spot. The park is a large stretch of meadows, sports fields, a dog park, and shoreline along the northwestern edge of Lake Washington. I head down the main road, across one of the parking lots, past a group of people playing ultimate frisbee, and down a trail that winds through the trees until it finally lets me out on the wide paved path that follows along the lake. The water is a perfect blue green, the sky light blue with wisps of cloud, the sun warming my shoulders.

People are already lining the lake's edge, a lot of them groups of kids our age. I head north until I see Kite Hill and the bathrooms right across from it, and I start looking for my friends.

"Hayley!" I whip my head around and see Kevin waving furiously at me from the lakeshore. I veer off through the grass and around people's blankets and he heads straight for me. It's not until I'm too close that I realize he's soaking wet.

I shriek, but he's already wrapping his long, skinny arms around me, giggling like an evil scientist.

"So cold!" I yell.

"Got 'em!" he crows.

"You're such a jerk," I say, grinning, as he releases me and runs away back into the water with a whoop.

I lay out my towel next to the others at the spot they've claimed and scan the shore. Kev and Bri are having a splash fight in the shallows, and I can see Jacob floating on his back a little farther out. But where's Talia? I squint out a little farther, and spot her, swimming back from the buoy.

Around us are several other groups, one of mostly boys, one a mix, and then a smaller group of girls farther down from us. I shade my eyes and try to look like I'm just casually observing the scene, not checking them out.

"Hayley! Get in here!" Kev yells.

"I have to put on sunscreen!"

"Well, hurry up!"

I pull off the shorts and T-shirt I'm wearing over my swimsuit, dig the sunscreen out of my bag, and start slathering it on. I don't want a repeat of last summer's early season burn.

The group of girls are chatting away about something, laughing every so often. Three of them are Black, one looks Latine, and one is white, as far as I can tell, and they're all wearing bright colors, like an array of sherbet ice creams. The white girl has green hair, and one of the Black girls has short-cropped curls and orange board shorts. Possible signs of gayness. Excellent. Although, the other girls could be gay or bi, too. And they might not be girls; they could be nonbinary, which is fine. I'm into nonbinary people, too. I know a lot of people don't think I'm queer when they look at me, just because I have long hair and don't dress alternative. But my style is queer because I'm a lesbian and I'm wearing it. And I wouldn't want to miss out on a potential date just because I assumed they were straight.

"Hi."

I look up at Talia and grin. "I saw you way out there."

She smiles, still breathing hard. "Yeah. Look at my new suit!"

The top is a light peach halter with a high neck, and the bottom is leopard print with a short skirt that skims the tops of her thighs. It took Talia a while to find a swimsuit style she felt comfortable in after coming out, and seeing her so happy in this one makes me smile, too. "It's so cute!"

"So is yours. Is that Ella's?"

I laugh. "Yeah. Mine didn't fit."

"Well, it looks great on you."

"Thanks."

"You wanna come chicken fight Kev and Bri with me?"

I look out into the water. Kev is waist deep, grinning at us, Bri sitting on his shoulders. They throw their arms out in a challenge.

"Oh, definitely."

After we lose three rounds of chicken to Kev and Bri, Talia and I take a break, stumbling out of the water and grabbing our towels. Jacob is already there, laid out on his stomach, and he opens one eye as we approach then closes it when he sees it's us. We settle in beside him, stretching out to let the sun warm us.

"Those fools," I say, watching Bri and Kev splash each other furiously.

"I swear, Kev is an ADHD king," Talia says.

"I can see that." I look back toward the group of girls I was scoping before. A few more have joined. I nudge Talia and jerk my head in their direction.

"Oh yeah." She scans the group casually, as if she's observing the whole beach, then back to the lake. "They're cute."

My eyes gravitate to the Latine girl. She was wearing a T-shirt dress earlier, but now she's taken it off to reveal a rainbow-striped bikini. Classic. Two of the other girls are definitely cuddling.

The whole group looks so cool. I can hear bits of their music floating toward us over the noise of the people around us, and I'm pretty sure they're playing Megan Thee Stallion.

I look away, out to the water. Kev and Bri fade and all I can see is me and Rainbow Bikini splashing each other and giggling. She jumps on me, wrapping her legs around my waist, and we both go under. When we surface, coughing and laughing, I grab her and pull her close for a cold, wet kiss.

We'd be so cute together.

"You're swooning." Talia's voice jerks me back to reality.

"Nuh-uh," I say.

She laughs. "You did that sigh you always do when you're daydreaming about a girl."

"I—" I can't even deny it. I didn't hear myself sigh, but she's probably right. I'm so obvious.

"What about you?" I ask.

She shades her face and glances over at the group again. "I don't know. They're all cute. I like those orange board shorts."

"What about the person wearing them?"

Talia screws up her mouth. "I mean, she's cute? I don't know anything about her, though."

I shrug. "She looks so fun. She keeps trying to toss a grape into that other girl's mouth. And her laugh is really bubbly."

Talia tilts her head at me. "How is this so easy for you?"

I laugh. "I don't know. I just see someone and I can imagine all our possibilities. It's like a movie in my head."

Talia nods and looks out at the water again, but her eyebrows come down ever so slightly. I open my mouth to ask her what's up.

But we're interrupted by Kev and Bri running up to us. Kev shakes himself like a dog, spattering us all with water. We all shriek and throw up our hands as he laughs.

"I'm hungry!" he says.

Bri breaks out the snacks. Chips, candy, crackers, and a grocery-store veggie platter go into the center of our little circle, along with some hummus, ranch dip, and LaCroix from the tiny cooler. I grab a can and crack it open, relishing the first bubbly sip. It's the key lime flavor, or "Skittle water," as we like to call it. My favorite.

"So." Jacob rolls over and reaches for the chips. "You two see anyone who catches your fancy yet?" He flutters his eyelashes dramatically.

"That group over there." I nod in the direction of the girls. Some of them are in the water now. Our friends all turn to look at the same time. "You guys!"

They all turn back around.

"Sorry!" Bri hisses.

"We're trying to find dates, not creep people out." I press my hand to my forehead.

"What about you, Talia?" Bri asks.

"I don't know." Talia twists her mouth. "There are people I think are cute, but I don't know if I want to talk to any of them. I don't understand flirting at all."

"Oh my god, *same*," Bri says.

"Really?"

"Yes! God, if Karina hadn't done what she did, we would never have dated," Bri said. We all nod. We know the story: Bri was representing our school at a debate competition last spring, and Karina was the other school's rep. She beat Bri, but afterward, came right up to them and said it was hard to concentrate the whole time because of how cute Bri was. They'd started texting, had their first date soon after, and now they're girlfriends.

"I wish everyone was that direct," Talia says. "Or that more people were fine with me being direct."

"Well, this is kind of a test run, anyway," I remind her. "It's OK if we don't find anyone today."

"What about the lists?" Jacob says.

We both look at each other and laugh. "We're waiting on that for now," I say.

"Too much pressure," Talia adds. I reach out and squeeze her arm, and she smiles at me. We're always on the same page.

"So Bri . . ." Kev trails off, grinning. "How *is* Karina?"

"Oh, um." Bri blushes and looks down at their towel. "She's fine."

"That's all?" Kev nudges them, and we all watch as a smile breaks out on their face.

"I really like her," they say softly.

Jacob squeals. I grin. I love seeing my friends happy, especially when romance is involved.

"Tell them about your date the other day," Kev says. I know he and Bri are pretty tight.

"OK." Bri presses their hands to their cheeks, grinning fiercely down at their towel. We all lean forward, ready for the details. "So she really likes doing activities for our dates and all those kind of typical romantic things—flowers, surprises, picnics, stuff like that. Sometimes I feel bad because I just don't really think that way. But anyway, she knows I get kind of stuck on thinking of things to do, so the other day I showed up at her house and she'd planned a whole day for us, and it was all my favorite things. It wasn't a surprise because she knows surprises make me anxious. But we went to Carkeek Park and looked for cool rocks, and then she took me to lunch at my favorite cafe in the U-District, and then we went to the used bookstore nearby and I got to show her all the comics I like! And then we went back to her house and watched cartoons all evening, and we made out—" they whisper the last words, and we all squeal. They flap their hands at us, and we fall silent. "Anyway, yeah. It was perfect."

"Oh my gosh." I put my hands over my heart. "That is *so* romantic."

They make eye contact with me, then look back down, still grinning. "I know."

"Y'all are about to be in loooooove," Kev says.

They smack his shoulder. "Can we talk about something else now?"

"Like the fact that Talia and Hayley are here to find dates and haven't hit on anyone yet?" He grins at us.

"It's a test run!" We say at the same time, and he just shakes his head, laughing.

We stay at the beach late, until the sun goes down and it's too chilly to swim anymore. As we gather our things, I can feel the warmth coming off my skin. I'm definitely burnt in spite of the sunscreen, but it was worth it.

At the park exit, we hop on a bus up to the University District. We're all starving, but I'm too jazzed from time with my friends to feel hangry.

Once we get to the Ave, the main street by the University of Washington, we make a beeline for Vietnamese food—banh mis, specifically. They're the perfect sandwich for a warm night, filling and savory.

We wander up and down the Ave, people-watching and making fun of all the college students who are already drunk. It feels like we're in a movie, like the perfect start to summer. Especially for a summer of love. The breeze is cool, but not cold, and the air smells like flowers. And car exhaust, because the street is busy. And occasionally weed.

I'm still not sure what else to add to my girlfriend list, but that's OK. I'll figure it out. For now, I just want to have fun and get over Sherika. I want to look at cute people, and maybe get a few social media handles, and see what happens from there. Maybe I'll find something like what Bri and Karina have. They're so perfect together.

Tonight was just the start. And it's totally fine that neither of us talked to anyone. Really.

We have the whole summer to find our people.

CHAPTER FIVE

T HAT WEEKEND, I get special dispensation to skip Sunday brunch for a very important occasion: Pride. The big parade happens downtown and starts at eleven, so I'm up earlier than usual. After pounding down some cereal, I'm digging through my closet for the perfect outfit. I need something that screams I'M GAY AND SINGLE to every girl in a ten-block radius.

I end up settling on high-waisted acid-wash denim shorts, a cropped tank top with multicolor stripes, and my white Converse. I put my hair up into a high bun and pop in my favorite earrings: a white ceramic cloud and a gold lightning bolt. The mismatch looks super queer. I smile at myself in the full-length mirror on the back of my closet door. I love being femme. That word, *femme*—ever since I came across it last year on one of my favorite queer websites, it's been an anchor in my chest, something reminding me that the way I dress and talk, the way I am in the world—is powerful.

Oh, right. One more thing. I carefully draw perfect wings of black eyeliner.

I'm gay and single. Look out, ladies.

"Hayley! Talia's here!" My mom shouts up the stairs. I grab my gold mini-backpack and stuff it with my wallet, phone, keys, granola bars, sunscreen, and water.

"Do you have—" Mom starts as I shoot past her toward Talia.

"Totally prepared! It's all in the backpack! Bye!" I grab Talia's hand and pull her after me.

I am *ready!* The sky is blue, the breeze is cool, the sun is warm. Perfect for Seattle Pride! I have so much energy. I drop Talia's hand and skip ahead of her down the sidewalk while she laughs.

"I think this is the most alert I've ever seen you in the morning," she says, catching up to me.

"Oh my god. Your romper!"

Talia grins and makes a ta-da motion with her arms. The romper is sleeveless and dark teal-green and printed all over with tiny cartoon rainbows. Talia's curls are down, blowing in the breeze, with her bangs and longer strands on either side framing her face. She's wearing neon pink lipstick.

"You look so cute," I say. She really does.

She smiles. "I mean, you too."

I tilt my head. "And something looks . . . wait. Did you get new glasses?"

"I diiiiiid," she sings out. Her old ones were thicker-framed; these are wire-rimmed, gold, and round. They open up her whole face and light up her brown eyes. That might also be the sun catching them though.

"They look so good."

"Why, thank you." She flips her hair. We smile at each other, and a bubble of happiness swells in my chest.

We talk the whole way to the light rail station. Talia and I both live in the Central District, closer to Capitol Hill, so we're going to catch the train going into downtown. Kev is taking the bus from farther south in the neighborhood to meet us. Bri, Karina, and Jacob are coming from the University District on the train, and we're going to try and time it to get on the same one.

Just as we arrive at the station, Bri texts us. They're on the train, coming our way.

"Where's Kev?" I look around wildly, and then I see him waving frantically as he weaves through the crowded sidewalk toward us.

We all tap our Orca cards and run down the stairs as fast as we can. The station platform is filled with people covered in rainbows, holding signs, laughing with each other. I see older lesbians kissing, chubby gay men holding hands, clumps of other teens chattering away.

First car, Bri texts the chat.

The train pulls in and we race through the crowd to keep pace with the front until it pulls to a stop. I scan the windows and—

"There!" I see them pressed against the second set of doors, making faces, dancing up and down. We dodge in ahead of a big group, almost stumbling over each other, piling toward the middle of the train as everyone presses in to make room for the people boarding.

"Happy Pride!" we all chorus at each other as the train zooms through the dark tunnel.

"Happy Pride!" Someone I read as a butch lesbian grins at us.

Someone else whoops it from down the car, and the whole crowd cheers and laughs.

I love this feeling. I'm part of something: a community, a history. I belong. We're all together, celebrating each other, what it took to be here.

I love being queer.

When we exit from Westlake Station downtown, the street is already packed. We link hands and weave our way slowly down the sidewalk. The crowd is thickest near the parade fencing along the curb, so we stay to the opposite side as much as possible, where there's more space to move.

I'm fourth in our little caravan, so I just let myself get pulled along. Kev's the tallest, and I can see him up front, head on a swivel, looking for a spot along the route. I look around at everyone. There are so many beautiful people everywhere, so many smiling faces, so much glitter-covered skin and outfits I could never pull off—or wouldn't be allowed to wear at all. My parents are open-minded, but they'd probably draw the line somewhere.

I catch eyes with a girl leaning against a café wall. She smiles at me—cute button nose and blue eyes—but it's too late, we're already being pushed along in the swirling current of people. Damn. But I made significant eye contact. That's something.

Our group makes a hard right turn, and Kev pulls us into the perfect spot against the fencing. There's enough space for Bri, Karina, and Jacob to be in front, and for the tall kids—me, Talia, and Kev—to stand behind them.

"Yuh! We're here!" Karina does a dance move, then leans over and kisses Bri.

"And just in time," Jacob yells over the sudden roar of motorcycles. He pops his noise-canceling headphones in and flaps his hands wildly, grinning.

This is the moment I live for.

Down the street they come, in slow advancing circles, the growl of hundreds of motorcycles echoing around us.

The Dykes on Bikes.

I see silver-haired butches on Harleys with their femmes seated behind them; a woman with long hair just like mine on a motorcycle that looks like a Transformer and has a trans pride flag on the back; a butch couple on a bright blue touring bike; all of them looping around and around down the street while the crowd screams over the roar of engines. I jump up and down, smiling so hard my cheeks hurt, cheering until my voice gets ragged. Talia catches my eye and we grin at each other, grabbing hands and bouncing together. I'm so happy I can't stand it, so happy I feel like I'm going to burst into tears. Pride season is my favorite season.

The parade is long, with everyone from small businesses to nonprofits to community groups to corporations with their own contingent. We collect pronoun pins from Planned Parenthood, brochures about health services from the local community center Gay City, and rainbow animal paw stickers from the Humane Society. We scream for a gaggle of drag queens and burlesque performers blasting Lady Gaga from their float. We clap for swing dancers and a hip-hop troupe, gasp at a martial arts demonstration, and stare curiously at the Leather Pride contingent.

When a big collective of kids from queer student groups across Seattle Public Schools walks by, we scream for stickers and one of the boys runs over. He hands all of us one, and when he gets to Kevin, he kisses the back of Kevin's hand before running back to the group.

We all exclaim at once, turning to him. He's grinning ear to ear. Kevin is pansexual—he came out to us last year. I've never seen him flirt with anyone, and he hasn't talked about crushes, but right now he's lit up like the summer sun.

"Maybe we should include you in the strategy," I tease.

"I'm good," he says, waving me off, but the smile stays on his face for a while.

Several hours in, boredom overtakes us, so we fight through the crowd to the next street over and head for Seattle Center. It's a big plaza with a huge fountain in the center, surrounded by lawns and walkways, and on the outer perimeter is an arena, a stadium, some performing arts venues, a museum, and a food court. There are other businesses, too, but we head for the fountain like we do every Pride.

The fountain is a deep concrete bowl with a rim of seating around the edge and a giant silver ball at the center. Water shoots out of the ball in giant pulsing arcs, set to a song I can barely hear over the noise of the crowd and music from the stages set up on the surrounding lawns. We pile our stuff together and run down the sloping interior of the bowl, right up to the fountain and smack against it, screaming and laughing. The water is cold, and we dance under the sprays. Talia grabs my hand and twirls me around.

Finally, we all stumble out, back to our stuff, and sit panting on the fountain's edge. All around us are people doing the same thing, playing in the water, warming themselves on the rim. The hot sun beating down keeps us from getting too cold.

After a while, we migrate to a spot on the grass, laying out to let our clothes dry. Kev sprawls out with his eyes closed; Jacob breaks out the *Magic* cards and duels Bri while Karina looks on; Talia and I people-watch while munching on the chips Kev brought.

There are a lot of cuties, and a lot of them look our age. I point a few out to Talia, but she's doubtful.

"No pot leaves as fashion sense," she says, shuddering.

And—"She looks too bro-ey for me."

And—"Eh, I don't know, I don't really find them attractive."

"Talia!" I throw my hands up. "Who *is* your type, then?"

"You're not finding anyone either," she points out, grinning.

"OK, fine." I roll my eyes. "I'll go talk to . . ." I scan the crowd. *There.*

Someone I read as a girl is standing on the edge of the fountain next to a pile of bags, bouncing on the balls of her feet. She swivels slowly, watching the crowd and . . . wow. She's cute. Her round face is covered in freckles, and now I notice they cover the rest of her body, too, at least the skin I can see. Her hair is short in the back with a longer swoop of hair on top. She closes her eyes and turns her face up to the sun.

"Her!" I point.

"OK." Talia nods.

I sit there.

"Go do it, then." Talia purses her lips and arches an eyebrow.

"I'm going!" I jump up and head over before I can second-guess myself.

The girl opens her eyes as I approach.

"Hey," I say, waving.

". . . Hi?" She tilts her head to the side.

"Wanna go in the fountain with me?"

She glances down at the water. "Nah, I don't really like the whole fountain thing."

"Maybe I could help with that." I grin and twirl my hair. I actually twirl it. Like I'm in some fifties movie trying to seduce her. *Where is this coming from?*

And . . . she laughs.

It's a short, surprised cackle, and she stops herself, but it's too late. I want to sink into the ground and disappear.

"I'm sorry!" she says. "I thought you were straight."

"Oh." I should probably say something else, but her words are like a bolt to my chest.

She grimaces. "Oh man. I shouldn't have said that. That's dumb. We're at Pride. Of course you're not."

"Oh, it's fine!" I say in a high-pitched voice, but it's most definitely not fine. "I mean, a lot of straight people go to Pride, too!"

Why am I digging this hole deeper?

"Hey, baby," someone says, and we both look behind her to see a girl with short, spiky hair and a nose piercing coming up out of the fountain. She smiles at me. "Who are you?"

"No one!" I say, before the other girl can interject. "Have a good day."

I zip away, back to Talia, whose eyes are wide. I plop down in front of her, keeping my back to the girl. It feels like my face is on fire, and it's definitely not sunburn-related.

"She has a girlfriend," I say in a low voice.

"Damn."

"And she thought I was straight. She laughed at me."

"What?" Talia straightens up. I tell her the details and she shakes her head. "That's so dumb. You don't look straight."

"I don't know." I swallow. "You know me, so you know I'm

not. But the rest of the world doesn't." Of course this happened. Of course I got rejected. I can feel the tears welling up but I don't want to cry in front of everyone.

"I mean, what does it even mean to look straight?" Talia says, throwing up her hands.

I nod. I know logically there isn't one way to be queer or look queer. And part of me believes it. But part of me really doesn't. I want to have a girlfriend, but what if I'm missing out because they're missing *me*? If I changed the way I look, would they see me as a possibility?

I wonder again about my hair. I've been thinking about cutting it. And maybe that would help. If I had short hair, if I had a piercing, too, if I didn't look so. . .

I don't finish the sentence in my head, but I don't have to. I hate that I'm even almost thinking it. This morning I felt so confident in my look, in myself, and with just one comment, it's gone. Talia watches me with a half-outraged, half-sympathetic expression. I blow out a big sigh and lay back onto the grass, closing my eyes against the bright sun and the tears that still want to fall.

I thought the summer love strategy was a sure thing. That Talia and I would crack the code together. But I feel even worse than I did when Sherika got with Trey.

This sucks.

At home that night, before I shower off all the sweat and glitter, I stand in front of the mirror, staring at my hair. It's the same as it's been for the past year: elbow-length, with bangs that get in my eyes now if I don't push them to the side or part them in the middle. The only change I've made recently was dying it pink a few months ago, and now the dye is faded to barely more than a tint. I've wanted it this long for years, but I've been feeling bored with it lately. And the girl's laugh is still echoing in my head, her words repeating over and over: *I thought you were straight! I thought you were straight! I thought you were straight!*

For some reason, an image pops into my head. Me, in sixth grade, hiding in the bathroom, trying not to have a panic attack.

I can't believe I put myself out there and let myself feel this way.

"I am *not* straight!" I tell the mirror and glare at myself. It's time for a change.

I grab my phone and crank up my pump-up playlist. Digging through the bathroom drawers, I find scissors.

I tilt my head, pursing my lips at my reflection. How short do I want to go? Should I go asymmetrical? I really like that short haircut a lot of actresses have now, with the long top they can sweep to the side, and the shorter back that's not buzzed but just enough to grab with your fingers.

Yes. That's what I'm going to do.

I separate my hair into two parts, tying the top up in a bun with my bangs. I gather the rest of my hair on the bottom into a ponytail. Deep breath.

Snip.

OK. That's not bad. It's choppy against the back of my neck, but still too long. The quiet metallic swish of the scissors makes my scalp tingle as I clip away more hair, pulling chunks away from the back of my head with my fingers and cutting them. It's probably uneven, but I'll fix it later once I've got the basic bones of the haircut.

When the back feels short enough, I look at myself in the mirror, turning my head side to side. It looks pretty good. Maybe I have a future as a hairstylist. Maybe a stylist to the stars.

I shake off a brief daydream where I'm cutting Kristen Stewart's hair and she's giving me dating advice and look at the bun. It's time.

Snipping the bun feels a lot more intimidating. Once I do this, my hair will be gone. No turning back.

It's fine, though. The most important thing is that no one will tell me I look straight.

Hopefully.

Even though straight women have short hair, too . . .

"Shut up, brain," I hiss at myself in the mirror. I slide the hair tie off, holding the hair bunched in my hand, and pull my hand away from my head, figuring out the length I want on top.

Snip.

It's done.

I look at myself, or at least, I try to—hair is falling in my face. I push it back, running my fingers through it.

It just kind of . . . lies there. It doesn't look cool and choppy and effortless like Kristen Stewart's hair. It just looks like a big mass of hair. Uneven. Shapeless. The ends blunt and way too obvious where I clipped them.

I close my eyes and take a deep breath. It's OK. It's fine. I'm probably just tired. I'll take a shower, and in the morning it'll look better.

CHAPTER SIX

SPOILER ALERT: MY hair does not, in fact, look better in the morning.

I'm up at eight for practice, and after I stumble into the bathroom and wash the eye crusties away, I look at myself in the mirror.

"Oh no," I murmur.

This is bad.

Really bad.

My hair looks like a bowl cut and a broom had a baby on top of my head. The shorter parts stick out at all different lengths, even after I comb them down, even though I made sure to dry my hair completely before I went to sleep last night. And the cool, long, effortless swoop on top? It's a shapeless mass that poofs above my horrified face.

"Hayley!" Ella pounds on the door.

I grit my teeth and open it.

"Holy shit!" Her eyebrows fly up. "What did you do?"

"What does it look like?" I brush past her, as if it's fine, nothing's wrong, I totally meant to look like this.

She just laughs and shuts the bathroom door behind her.

I toss my pride aside and run back to my room, scrabbling through my tangled bedding until I find my phone.

"Talia!" I screech as soon as she picks up my FaceTime. I put my face close to the screen so she can't see my hair.

"Ow! Too loud."

"Sorry, sorry." I lower my voice to a whisper. "Talia. I fucked up."

"What did you do?"

"I cut my hair."

"You got a haircut?"

"No."

She's silent, looking at my face.

"I did it," I say. "I cut it. Last night. With scissors. In the bathroom."

She nods, mouth twitching, but she keeps her face serious. "I understand the gravity of the situation, so I am resisting the urge to make a *Clue* joke right now."

"I appreciate your restraint," I say. The *Clue* board game and movie was one of Talia's special interests as a kid. For a while, whenever anyone asked a question that sounded even remotely like "Who did this?" she'd answer, "Colonel Mustard, in the ballroom, with the revolver." I know how much effort it must take for her to hold back right now.

"How can I help?" she asks.

"I need to go to a salon. Or barbershop. Or wherever they cut hair. After practice. Fuck, Sherika is going to see my awful hair."

"Rudy's," she says immediately. "On Capitol Hill. That's where my mom takes me. I always see gay people there."

"Perfect."

"I'll meet you there after your practice," she says. "Don't worry, we'll fix this."

I hide my hair under a baseball cap before I leave the house and keep it on when I get to the gym. I do not feel cute, and I do not want Sherika—or anyone else on the team—to see me like this. I'm hoping I can get away with the cap, and as the first few girls arrive, no one says anything.

"Hayley!" Mariah's voice echoes across the gym floor just as I go up for a shot.

My arms jerk and the ball clanks off the backboard. Big miss. I turn around and her head is tilted, eyes scanning my face. "Where's your hair?"

"In the trashcan at my house," I say.

She cackles. "I could have figured that out."

"Oh my gosh!" Anh's made her way over, eyes wide. "Your hair!"

"All gone!" I force a smile.

"Are you OK? Is this a cry for help?" She narrows her eyes.

"No, no! I'm fine. Don't joke about that."

"Sorry. You've just had long hair for, like, forever." Anh and I weren't really friends in middle school, but we got put together for group projects a few times. She was always kind to me, even when other kids weren't.

I shrug. "I just wanted a change."

"Then why are you wearing a hat?" Mariah arches an eyebrow.

I glance around. No one is looking at us, so I sweep it off my head and strike a pose. Mariah and Anh both flinch.

"I'm getting it fixed after practice," I say, my grin feeling more like a grimace.

"I'd hope so." Mariah shakes her head, smirking. "Sherika see you yet?"

"Mariah!" I reach out and swat her arm. "She'll hear you."

We both glance over. Sherika is stretching on the sidelines, her long legs gleaming under the lights. She looks up, notices us, and waves, smiling that wide, gorgeous smile. I wave back and hear Mariah snicker behind me.

"You're such a simp for that girl," she murmurs.

"Shut up." I hiss, glaring at her. She bats at me, I bat at her, and then we're in a slap fight.

"Ladies!" All three of us jump, turning in unison at a voice we know too well. Coach Kay is standing there, arms crossed, but her eyes are crinkled in amusement. She's tall and broad, a former center. She's wearing her usual track pants and T-shirt, her white skin sunburned. "I'm glad to see practice is going well."

"Yes. Yeah. It's going great, Coach," I say. "We were just getting started."

"Wonderful." She holds up a sheaf of paperwork. "I had these to do, and it felt like a good reason to get out of the house and see how y'all are doing down here. Hayley, are you in charge this summer?"

I nod. "Sherika's been leading the practices with me."

"Good. She knows a lot. She'll be a good mentor." Coach smiles at me. *Am I imagining things or do her eyes pause on my hair?* "OK, don't let me distract you. Have fun."

"Thanks!"

She heads across the gym to her office, exchanging high fives with some of the players along the way. I pull the baseball cap back on.

"*She'll be a good mentor?*" Mariah murmurs. "Sherika's varsity captain. You know what that means?"

"No, what?" I check to make sure my hair is completely hidden. Nobody else can see this disaster.

"I bet Coach has her eye on you to move up this year."

"No way." I wave her off.

"Don't make me slap you again." Mariah heads off to the sidelines to drop her bag. "Are we getting this thing started or what?"

Anh follows after her, walking backward, giving me a meaningful look.

I widen my eyes back and turn to the gym, calling out for everyone to circle up. As I do, a tingle of excitement runs through me. If Mariah's right, I don't want to give Coach any reason to doubt me. I'm going to make these practices the best they can possibly be.

When I get to Rudy's after practice, baseball cap firmly in place, Talia is already there. She hugs me.

"Everything's going to be OK," she says solemnly.

I nod, and we head inside.

Rudy's is cool—in both temperature and aesthetic. The floor is concrete with a row of leather swivel chairs in front of a mirror that runs the length of one of the walls. Concert posters are plastered all over the other black walls. It's quiet. One man is getting his hair faded in the far chair by a hairstylist with a bright red mullet, and a girl our age is reading in one of the lobby chairs by the window.

The receptionist smiles as we walk up. They're wearing a denim vest with a giant pronoun pin on the collar. "Hello! What can I do for you today?"

Talia looks at me.

I reach up and slowly pull off my cap. "I cut my own hair and I need someone to . . ." I gesture at my head, my face heating up.

The receptionist must see this all the time because they don't laugh; they don't even raise an eyebrow. "Of course! Have a seat over there and we'll get you in as soon as he's done. Shouldn't take long."

I pull the hat back on. "Thanks."

We sit a few seats down from the girl, and Talia glances at her. "That's such a good book."

The girl lifts her head. "Hmm?" She's got a heart-shaped face, bright teal eyeshadow, and short hair that looks professionally done. I pull my cap down a little tighter.

"Your book." Talia gestures at it. "*Simon vs. The Homo Sapiens Agenda*? It's one of my faves."

"Oh! Yeah!" The girl looks at the book and then smiles at Talia. "I've never read it before. But I really like it so far."

"You've never read it?"

"I know." The girl grimaces. "It came out forever ago. I've always heard about it but never got around to it."

"Oh no, I'm not judging!" Talia waves her hands. "I'm just excited you get to experience it for the first time."

Talia's face is definitely redder than a few seconds ago. *Is she . . . blushing?*

The girl puts the book down and tilts her head, smiling back. "That's a really cool thing to say. People usually just make fun of me for living under a rock."

"I mean, I think rocks are pretty cool."

They smile at each other and just sit like that for a moment, looking at each other. Is Talia . . . flirting?

Is that girl flirting back?

"I'm Rose. They/them." *OK, not a girl.*

We introduce ourselves and our pronouns and chat as we wait for my stylist to be free. Rose goes to the alternative school downtown, and they have the style to match: ripped black jeans, platform Doc Martens, and a cool denim vest covered in pins. Talia comments on the pins, and Rose stands up and twirls around, showing the vest off more. I spot various nerdy references as well as a nonbinary pride flag, and on the back is a big patch of a constellation.

"It's Leo. My sun sign." They grin. "What are your signs?"

Talia smiles. "We actually have the same birthday. We're both Cancers."

"Oh my god! So many feeeeeelings."

Talia laughs. "I guess so."

Rose and Talia keep chatting about astrology, and then about constellations in general, and then astronomy. When Talia finds out that Rose loves astronomy too, her whole face lights up.

"That was a *major* special interest of mine!"

"No way!"

"Yes. I've never met another person my age who's so into it."

And then they're off, talking about Stephen Hawking and black holes and a lot of other things I haven't heard Talia talk about in years. I'm not really part of the conversation anymore, just watching it happen. Meeting someone randomly at a salon after I butcher my hair definitely wasn't part of the strategy, but Talia's handling this like a pro.

And they're really talking now. Talia's whole body is turned toward them, and Rose is waving their hands about whatever subject they're on, but my ears are fuzzing out. It feels like I've stopped existing to both of them.

I'm being so petty. I should be happy for Talia. The strategy is working. She's having a meet-cute right in front of me. Her phone is out, and so is Rose's, and they're exchanging social media handles.

I take a few deep breaths. This is fine. I'm going to find my person, too. It's not a bad thing that it's taking me a little longer.

"You ready, kiddo?" A new voice shakes me out of my anxiety spiral. The man in the chair—Rose's dad, I guess—is standing there. Rose says goodbye to both of us.

"I'll DM you later," they say, giving Talia finger guns.

Talia laughs. "Sounds good!"

"Hayley?"

I look over and the hairstylist smiles at me. "I heard you have a haircut you'd like touched up."

"Yes! Yeah." I stand up and follow her to the chair. Talia just got contact info for a cutie. *That's fine. It's good! The strategy is working.*

It's totally fine.

When the stylist finishes, she spins me around to look in the mirror.

"What do you think?"

My jaw drops. "Wow!"

I don't know what magic she worked, but the fluffy mess on my head has been transformed into a sleek, short pixie cut, blonder now that everything is properly layered and trimmed. It's not what I was going for when I picked up the scissors last night—it's better. My cheekbones pop. I look older, like the cool, confident college girls I've seen striding through the University District. I turn my head side to side.

"This is amazing!" I run my hands over the back of it. My hair feels so soft. "Thank you so much."

"You're so welcome." She smiles at me.

As we leave the salon, I skip ahead of Talia. The breeze ruffles my hair, and I can feel every little change in air pressure as it does. There's no hair lying heavy down my back, sticking to my neck. I feel so light and free.

"You look so good," Talia says, watching me.

"I know, right?" I twirl around in the middle of the sidewalk, almost bumping into some business dude in a suit who ducks, glaring at me. Talia and I speedwalk away, giggling.

"So, um . . ." Talia pulls out her phone. "Rose DM'd me."

"Oh!" It all comes back in a rush. I was so caught up in the excitement about my hair that I forgot about Talia's success. "You got their social?"

Talia looks at me funny. "You saw me do that."

Yes. Yes, I did. In the middle of my spiral.

"Ugh, sorry. I kinda zoned out."

"It's all good." Talia shows me the DM. "Did I do OK?"

I look at the message from Rose: it was so fun talking to you! what was that book you mentioned?

Talia replied with a link to the book and then said: Same! What are your plans the rest of the week?

"That seems like a good follow-up!" I squeeze her arm. "You did it. You got someone's social. How does it feel?"

She blushes. "I don't know. It's cool? They seem sweet. And we have things in common, which is nice."

"See?" I nudge her. "I knew you'd find someone cool." The petty feeling is gone, and it's a relief. I'm happy for Talia. And maybe with this cool new haircut, I'll meet someone, too.

"I guess." She looks down at her phone again, at the DM, and a small smile curls the corners of her lips. "You wanna get food?"

"Always."

CHAPTER SEVEN

WHEN I CHECK my phone after practice the next day, I see a text from Kev in the group chat: So what's the next step in the strategy?

I open the thread and scroll through the usual videos and memes that I missed during basketball 'til I get to his text, and as soon as I do, a reply from Talia pops up.

The pool, she says.

Oh yeah. The outdoor one right? When? How we getting there? His texts come rapid fire, each sentence in a new one. He's the double—no, quadruple—texter of the group. Though I'm not one to talk.

Kev you are wayyyy too peppy rn, I type back.

Lmfao mom got us coffee this morning before Parker's surgery, he says.

OMG! That was this morning?!

Yaaaa. Everything went good. We're already home. They're totally out of it. It's hilarious.

I know Parker must be happy now that their top surgery is done, and Kev, too—even though it's a pretty straightforward procedure, he was still a little nervous about whether they would be OK. I send a celebratory string of emojis, and the others chime in with congrats and well wishes.

We were wondering if your mom could maybe drive us in the van? Talia asks after the celebration GIFs have tapered off.

Ohhhh, Kev says. Idk. Depends on stuff with Parker. I might be in rotation to take care of them. What day?

We all haggle over scheduling for a little bit. Talia's family planned a trip for the coming Fourth of July weekend, so we can't do then. Bri is going to the same art camp as Sam—they're just in a different class for their age level—so they can only do things after three during the week. But finally, we land on Wednesday afternoon next week.

I put it in my Google calendar so I won't forget, then send a selfie I took yesterday to show off my new haircut. Everyone showers me with compliments, which makes me feel even better about my new look. I can't wait to accessorize it with big earrings.

As the bus rattles through the University District, it starts to fill up with students getting out of summer classes. I don't know why anyone would voluntarily go to school during the summer, but maybe it's different once you get to college. Maybe if you're studying something you actually care about, you actually want to be at school.

There're a couple groups of kids my age, too. The University District isn't only a college kid haunt; the Ave is wall-to-wall restaurants, coffee shops, and shops selling everything from secondhand clothing to books to New Age spiritual accessories. My friends and I hang out there sometimes, wandering in and out of stores, and I'm guessing that's what these groups were doing, too. One group all has bubble teas; the other has shopping bags with clothes peeking out the top.

Bubble Tea group is loud, sprawling across the seats at the very back of the bus. I'm sitting on the bench seat at the middle, facing the doors there, so I glance at the group from time to time. I can hear them through my headphones, but it doesn't bother me. They're obviously gay, with various pride pins on their bags and a few kids with brightly dyed hair. About half the group is Asian, with a couple white girls and two guys whose race I can't really tell.

One of the girls is gesturing wildly while she talks—clearly telling a story. As the others laugh and interrupt, another girl catches my eye. She's wearing a Harry Styles concert tee—good taste!—and sparkly silver Converse. She gives me a little smirk and eye roll, as if to say, *Oh my god, my friends are so extra*, and I make the face back.

When she turns back to her friends, I scan the small backpack she's wearing. There it is—the pansexual pride flag. My heart beats a little faster. We just made significant eye contact. And she's pan. And really cute.

She glances back at me. I feel the blush instantly, but she smiles, so I smile back. I guess she wasn't bothered by me staring.

One of her friends scans me up and down, then elbows her and whispers something in her ear. The girl snorts and shakes her head.

Ugh. My chest tightens, anxiety creeping in. I know I have no idea what they just said, but my mind is already filling in the blanks: her friend told her to go for it, and she's not interested. She's less than not interested—she's actively repelled by the idea.

I stare down at my phone, breathing through the anxiety, and when they all jump up to get off at their stop, I don't look up.

As the bus rattles away from the curb, I gaze out at the university buildings, but I'm not really seeing them. Talia is probably messaging Rose right now and hitting it off. It was so easy for her. She didn't even need the strategy. She met someone when we were just sitting in a salon.

I'm happy for her. She's my bestie and I love her, and I want her to find someone who knows how great she is. I just . . .

I thought this would be easier for me, too. I barely have to look at someone and I get a crush. But so far, I'm striking out again and again, and I don't know what I'm doing wrong.

The walk from the bus stop to my house is especially beautiful now that everything's in bloom, and I pause to sniff a few yellow roses on the massive climbing bush on the neighbor's fence. The girls on the bus keep popping into my mind, but I try to bat the thoughts away. Pansexual Girl is just one girl. There will be others.

That reminds me. Pool Day's coming up.

Once I'm home, I bound up the stairs and knock on the door to Ella's room.

She opens it. "Yes?"

"Can I borrow your suit again?"

She arches an eyebrow. "Um, no."

"Why not?"

"You didn't even wait for my answer last time before taking it, and you left it hanging wet on my door."

"I was running late! I didn't have time to wait for your answer." I cross my arms. "And it was wet because I handwashed it for you."

She rolls her eyes. "I don't care. You can't just take my stuff."

I groan. "Come on! You have a whole other suit!" But I can tell from the stubborn look in her eyes that she's not giving in.

"It's still mine, and I don't have to lend it to you if I don't want to! House rules, remember?" She shrugs, her face set in a smug expression that infuriates me. "Get your own."

I sigh. As annoying as it is—and as petty as she's being—Ella is right. When someone in the family sets a boundary, we have to respect it, even if we don't understand it. House rules.

"Fine." I glare at her. "See if I lend you anything from now on."

She shrugs and closes the door in my face.

I guess I'm going swimsuit shopping this week.

Talia needs alone time to save up her energy before she spends the weekend with her family, and nobody else feels like going shopping. I know I need to bring someone along so I don't get distracted and walk out with a bunch of new clothes instead of a swimsuit, so on Saturday, Mom and I take the light rail downtown. It's slightly embarrassing to be hanging out with one of my parents in public. But my mom actually has a sense of style and doesn't try to control what I wear for the most part, so it's OK.

"So, what are you thinking?" she asks as we flip through the racks at one of the department stores. "Seems like the high-waisted bottoms are still going strong."

"Yeah, I like that look. But I don't want to match them. I want like a patterned top and a solid color bottom or vice versa."

She pulls out a rainbow tie-dye top and teal bottoms, and I give a thumbs-up. The brighter the colors and louder the pattern, the better. I've never been known for my subtlety.

Fifteen minutes later, I'm heading into the fitting rooms with an armful of options. There's an item limit, so Mom stands outside the door and hands them over one at a time, taking my rejects in return.

Swimsuit shopping isn't my favorite thing, but it isn't my least favorite thing, either. Most of my friends hate it with a passion, which makes sense with dysphoria and other body-image issues. And it's just plain uncomfortable to stand in a room and look at yourself over and over while you decide whether the thing you're trying on is both comfortable enough to wear for hours and cute enough to allow other people to perceive you wearing it. That's the worst part for me. I always notice if what I'm wearing doesn't feel right—if it pinches too much, or the fabric is scratchy, or something about it is just off.

Finally, I find the one: a pink leopard-print top and metallic silver bottoms. It screams I AM A FEMME LESBIAN, and also, crucially, feels great to wear.

"This one!" I swing the door open and strike a pose for my mom, who claps dutifully.

"Hey, nice choice," a voice says, and I look over to the right. There's a girl standing there wearing the same suit, smiling at me.

"Hey! Yes! You too!" I finger-guns at her. *She's really cute. Did I just finger-guns?* I put my hands down immediately.

She's still smiling at me, and then— "Check this out!" Another girl emerges from a fitting room and does a twirl in a different suit.

Her attention shifts. "That looks so good!"

I shut the door and change quickly, replaying the moment over and over in my mind. *Was she flirting or was that just a compliment? Was it funny to her that we picked the same suit or does she think it's a good pick regardless? Does she think it looks good on me? Does that mean she finds me attractive?*

I grab the suit and rush out of the fitting room. I can't look at her. What if she's looking at me again? What if she's already back in her stall? It was probably nothing, just a compliment, and I'm not going to risk repeating what happened at Pride. And the bus. Summer love strategy? More like summer heartache strategy.

"Hayley!"

I stop short. I'm already up at the cash registers. *How did I get here?*

Mom speedwalks up beside me. "Slow down for a second. What's going on?"

"Nothing."

She raises an eyebrow. "I may be old, but I'm not oblivious."

I scuff my toe along the linoleum, making little squeaking sounds. I haven't told anyone in my family about the strategy yet. Not for any reason; it just hadn't come up, but I might as well now. "So me and Talia have this thing."

My mom is quiet. She's used to my tangents.

"After Sherika . . . we made up this whole plan. To help each other find girlfriends this summer. Or dates. They can be any gender; Talia's bi. Anyway, we came up with this strategy to go to all these places where people usually find love in movies, but I keep getting rejected, and it sucks."

Shoppers bustle around us, and my mom places a hand on my arm, guiding me gently out of the way into a nearby aisle. "I'm sorry, honey," she says.

"I don't know." I shrug. The nervous energy from my interaction with that girl is wearing off and now I just feel heavy. "That girl was cute, but I couldn't tell if she was flirting, and it was just so awkward."

"Oh, sweetie." Mom squeezes my arm. "You got nervous."

I nod, fiddling with the lipsticks lined up on the display next to us.

"You said this strategy includes going places. Where have you been going?"

I tell her about all the spots we'd picked, and our goals, and what happened at Pride. By the time I'm done, she's smiling.

"I love that idea!" She catches my look and changes course. "It's hard to get rejected, though. I didn't know that was why you cut your hair."

When my parents saw me after the salon, I'd played it off like I'd planned to do it. As far as I could tell, Ella hadn't said anything about seeing my disastrous attempt at self-styling. And Sam just looked at me and said it looked cool.

I shrug. "It's whatever."

"No, it's not. Listen, I know I'm just a run-of-the-mill straight lady, but that girl didn't know what she was talking about. I'm sorry she made that assumption about you."

"Thanks." I scuff one of my shoes against the linoleum floor.

"I know from what you've told me that there are a lot of ideas and opinions out there about what it means to look or be gay, but the only thing that matters is how you feel."

I wish it was that easy, that I could just flip a switch and not care about what other people think, but Mom's words feel good all the same. She opens her arms and I step into them for a hug.

"Shall we go get you that suit?" she says into my hair. "And maybe get some milkshakes on the way home?"

"Yes, please."

She gives me another tight squeeze, and then we head up to the cash register. I keep my eyes forward the whole way. I don't want to run into that girl.

CHAPTER EIGHT

B Y SOME MIRACLE, Wednesday is a perfect Seattle summer day. Clear blue sky, mid-seventies, with a slight breeze
that isn't too chilly. Sitting on our front porch that afternoon, I
breathe it in, closing my eyes. Kev and his mom snagged the others first, and they're picking me up in just a few minutes. Then
it's pool time.

I open my eyes. Our yard is small but lush with blooms,
thanks to Mom and Dad's gardening habit. The smell of lilacs
fills the air, and the roses are budding. Everyone else is already
gone for the day; it's just me and the sun. And my thoughts.

I've been practicing my breathing technique the last few days,
trying to take Mom's words in and let my anxiety pass through
me. The strategy doesn't have to be a source of stress. I can just let
it be fun and not take it too seriously. Who knows, today could
be the day! I can almost see her, the girl I might meet, splashing
in the blue-green water. Or them, the nonbinary cutie waiting
for me in the shallow end, because I'm not a good swimmer.

In my mind, I walk over to them. We start talking, and then:
laughter. They're laughing at me, and so are their friends, and so

is the whole pool, and I rush into the locker room even though my friends try to stop me.

I press a hand to my chest and rub right beneath my collarbone. Deep breaths. The pool is going to be fine.

"Hayley!"

I jerk my head up, and Kev's hanging out of the passenger seat window of his mom's van. Behind the tinted glass of the back seat, I can see the silhouettes of the others.

Kev grins. "Get in here."

I grin back and run to the van.

The pool we're going to is in West Seattle, a neighborhood that might as well be an island, that's how far it feels from the rest of the city. The bus route to the pool normally takes at least an hour or more, but driving, it takes half the time. We thank Kev's mom profusely when she drops us off.

"I'm going to go do some shopping and meet a friend back up on California," she says. California is one of the major streets in the neighborhood where a lot of the stores and restaurants are clustered. "Can you all be back out here in three hours?"

We chorus a yes, and she smiles. "Have fun and wear sunscreen."

Once we pay the fee and shower in our respective locker rooms—the men's, women's, and gender-neutral single-stalls—we meet poolside. This pool is different from other ones in Seattle: it's open-air, it's right on the beach, and instead of regular chlorinated water, it's heated seawater. No one in their right mind would take any more than the briefest of dips in the Puget

Sound, even in summer—it's way too cold—so this is the closest we can get.

This afternoon, the pool's teeming with other teenagers. We pick our way around groups sprawled out on towels and in folding chairs to a spot in the shade. I keep my eyes on my feet to avoid tripping over someone.

We lay out our own towels and sit down for the group sunscreen application ritual. Talia does my back while Jacob lets me do his. I try to be quick about it so he won't have to deal with the discomfort of touch too long. Bri and Karina take turns with each other, but they're weirdly quiet while they do it. Usually Bri is chattering about their latest feat in *Dungeons & Dragons*, or Karina is telling Bri about a funny video she saw. Today, though . . . nothing.

Huh.

I haven't noticed anything off between them. Maybe they're just tired today, and I'm being weird because I'm stressed. Bri and Karina are perfect together. Besides, Bri would tell us if something was going on.

Talia does Kev's back quickly, and then we're ready to go.

We all have to pass the swim test first—a crawl stroke across the pool and back—to prove we can handle leaving the shallow end. I try but barely make it halfway across. I have the stamina for it, thanks to basketball, but there's something about the coordination involved in swimming—moving the arms, kicking the feet, turning my head to breathe, actually breathing—and all the sensory input—water on my face! In my nose! Oh god,

I can't breathe!—that makes it impossible. Jacob doesn't even attempt it. He bobs with his feet firmly on the ground in the shallow end, smiling as I walk through the water toward him, still coughing saltwater out of my lungs.

"Shallow end crew!" he says and fist-bumps me. I clear my throat for hopefully the last time and laugh hoarsely.

I don't really mind the shallow end. One by one, the little kids go home for dinner, and our friends paddle back across every so often to check in with us. Jacob and I float by putting our hands down on the bottom of the pool and letting our legs drift out in front of us. It's so nice to be in the water. I tip my head back, letting the sun warm my face.

"Do you see anyone you like yet?" Jacob asks.

My eyes snap open. "Oh. Right."

He giggles, and I shake my head. "I'm not very good at this whole finding a girlfriend thing."

"I mean, how is one good at these things anyway?" He shrugs.

Talia already found someone, I want to say, but I don't know if she's told the group yet. And I don't want to sound bitter and jealous. I'm not either of those things. I don't know what exactly I'm feeling, but it doesn't feel good.

OK, maybe I'm a little jealous. It's just frustrating that we originally came up with this strategy to help me get over Sherika and somehow I'm still struggling. I don't even like Sherika that much anymore. Yeah, I still feel fluttery when she walks through the gym doors for practice every morning, but I don't think about her constantly like I did before.

I watch the groups of teenagers around us. A boy cannon-balls into the deep end, making a few girls shriek. A group of kids who look queer lounge in the sun, talking about a movie they clearly saw together, their conversation punctuated by bursts of laughter. Two boys sit on the edge of the pool, their pinkies linked, splashing their feet in the water. I smile at them, and they smile back.

I look over at Jacob. "Do you ever think about dating someone?"

"Sometimes. It's fun to think about. Holding hands, kissing, planning epic dates . . ." He grins dreamily. "OK, so maybe I think about it a lot. Romance is just so . . ." He wiggles and squeals, splashing his feet. I copy him and laugh, but not in a mean way. This is just one of the ways we communicate, and understanding each other this way feels good, makes me happy. Some things you can't express in words. Sometimes you need to move and make sounds to say what you really mean.

"Totally!" I say. "I feel like my heart's going to explode when I think about having a girlfriend."

He watches me, tilting his head a bit. "Do you think that's how love feels? Or is that just crush feelings?"

"Definitely crush feelings. But you feel that first, right? That's what bonds you to the other person. I think love probably feels the same, but different, too. Deeper, more solid, more calm?" I run my hand over the surface of the water.

Jacob hums, watching my hand. "Do you think Bri and Karina are in love?"

I look across the pool to find them. They're in the far corner, talking to each other, and they're not smiling. Talia and Kev are closer to us, horsing around. One of the lifeguards is eyeing them.

"I don't know," I say. "Bri hasn't said anything about that yet."

We watch our friends in silence. It's not awkward, though. Silence is never awkward with my friends, but especially not with Jacob. When I'm with him, we can communicate just in noises or be quiet for an hour and then say a few things, and it feels so natural. He also lets me monologue as long as I want about whatever thing I'm fixated on at the moment. He's not one of those people who gets annoyed because I'm telling him something he doesn't care about. He just asks me questions about it.

Talia's that way, too. I'm so lucky we grew up together, because for a long time, no one else would tolerate me. Any friend I made always got sick of me after a while. I was annoying, or self-involved, or a know-it-all, or just too much. I didn't know how to explain to them that I was just excited and wanted to share how excited I was. Or that I was trying to relate to them by telling them about something I'd experienced that was similar to what they were telling me. They didn't get it.

Talia does. Jacob does. All our friends do. Once I started hanging out with other neurodivergent people, life got a lot better.

"What about that person?" Jacob pokes my foot with his, and I look up. He jerks his head. "The rainbows."

Someone I read as a girl is standing in the shallows, her arms crossed on the concrete edge of the pool, talking to a group of kids sitting beside the pool. It looks like she's trying to get them to come in, but they're shaking their heads. She's really cute: short, with a buzzed head, rainbow board shorts, and sporty green top. She's got toned shoulders, and her skin is a dark, warm shade of brown. Butch babe energy.

She glances over and our eyes catch. I immediately look away at Jacob, who widens his eyes.

"She just looked at me," I hiss.

"I saw!" His eyes shift. "*Hayley.*"

"What?" My heart is racing all of a sudden, like a motor just kicked in.

"She's coming over here. Uh. Have fun!"

"*Jacob!*" I whisper, but he's already paddling away.

Oh my god. Oh my god. I take a deep breath and turn.

She's a few feet away, grinning at me, a cute smirky smile that lifts one corner of her perfect lips. *Stop staring at her lips, Hayley.* I look at her eyes. They're a deep, dark, gorgeous, calm brown.

"Hey there," she says. Her voice is husky.

"Hi!" *Could I be any squeakier?*

"I'm Mel. I saw you looking at me."

"Um. Yes. I was. I'm Hayley."

"My friends won't swim with me, and I don't want to swim alone." She glances in the direction Jacob went. "Seems like you're alone, too . . ."

"I am." I smile. "Wanna swim with me?"

"I do."

"Great."

"Sweet."

We grin at each other, and it feels like my chest is exploding.

I lose track of time entirely while hanging out with Mel. We exchange our pronouns and our ages, and she asks where I go to school.

"Jefferson," I say.

"Oh, the Salmon!" She splashes me and I shriek. "What you doing in the shallow end?"

"Shut up!" I splash her back, giggling. "You're here, too."

It turns out she goes to school in the south end, and our teams are rivals. "You play sports?" she asks, squinting at me.

"Basketball."

"Oh, thank god." She leans back and floats. "We can keep talking."

"What do you mean? Do *you* play sports?"

She puts her feet down on the bottom of the pool and flexes a toned bicep. "Soccer."

"I'd expect you to flex a leg for that, not an arm," I say.

"Oh, she's picky," Mel says, grinning, and raises one buff brown leg above the water, tensing her calf muscle. It bulges, and my eyebrows lift before I can stop myself. "Happy now?"

I shrug, smirking. "I guess."

Mel's dimple pops when I say that. I really like her smile. It's wide and pushes her round cheeks up, crinkling the corners of her eyes. My chest isn't exploding anymore—it's buzzing, like there's an electrical current between us. *Are we flirting?*

Seattle is full of transplants, but it turns out we're both from here. We compare notes on neighborhoods, all our schools, our favorite places in the city. There's a playful debate on Seattle sports teams—I favor the Storm, our women's basketball team, of course, and she's a die-hard fan of the Seahawks and the Sounders, our football and soccer teams—and then the conversation shifts to gender and sports, and then to the first queer movie we ever saw. We're in the middle of discussing the importance of queer and trans characters when someone calls her name, and we both look up.

"Stop flirting, we gotta go!" One of her friends stands poolside, hands on hips, shit-eating grin on their face. They wave at me. "Hi, cutie. She get your info already?"

"Oh my god." Mel makes a face at her friend. "I was *about* to!" She turns to me. "So, uh . . ."

"Let me get my phone." I smile.

We exchange information, and she says she'll DM me later. Says it was good talking to me. She turns back once before she disappears into the locker room and flashes me a peace sign. I wave back.

When I turn around, my friends are lined up at the edge of the pool, chins on the concrete edge, grinning up at me.

"Hi there." I side-eye them.

"You just got contact info," Jacob says.

"From that total babe," Kev adds.

"I'm so proud of you," Karina says solemnly.

Talia just grins at me.

Bri slow-claps, and they all join in. I shriek and cover my face, then slide into the water beside them.

"What do you think? Do you like..." Talia waits for pronouns.

"Her," I say.

"Do you like her? What's her name? Where does she go to school?"

"Her name is Mel, and she's at one of the schools in the south end. And yes, I like her. I mean. I just met her. But she seems really cool and confident, and she's super funny. She's a soccer player, and politically conscious, we talked about representation in media for, like, ever—"

"Hayley, you're *babbling*." Bri grins at me. "You liiiiike her!"

"Shut *up!*" I'm smiling so hard my cheeks ache.

They all tease me a little longer, and then Kev wants to cannonball off the high dive again, so they all follow him. Jacob gets out to chill on his towel with his noise-canceling headphones on, since he's getting overstimulated. Then it's just me and Talia left in the shallow end.

"I can't believe we both got dates!" I say, grinning at her.

"I mean, we don't have dates *yet*," Talia says.

"OK, yes, technically true."

"I've been DMing with Rose more, though." Talia smiles. "They're back from vacation next week and then we're gonna make plans."

"OMG!" I hold up a hand and we high-five. I'm not feeling any jealousy, just excitement for her, which is a huge relief. I want Talia to be happy. "Maybe we can go on a double date eventually."

"That would be cool." Talia smiles. Suddenly, she sweeps her hand through the water and splashes me.

I splutter and splash her back. "What was that for?"

"Just cause I could." She paddles away, and I slow-run after her through the water.

"Get back here!"

"Can't get me!" She sticks her tongue out.

"No splashing!" The lifeguard bellows through his bullhorn. We widen our eyes at each other and giggle.

"This is so exciting," I say, lifting my feet up and floating on my back, staring up at the perfect blue sky. "Talia and Hayley, dating at last."

Talia laughs and joins me, both of us buoyed in the warm salty water. A gull soars overhead and I take a deep breath. I feel like I could float forever.

CHAPTER NINE

WAKE UP THE next morning in a rush of excitement and just lie there, basking for a moment, taking it in. Mel and I, chatting in the pool, exchanging our info. The strategy is working. At least, that's if she messages me. She didn't last night, and the thought of another rejection is looming like clouds on the horizon of this perfect summer day.

The message notifications on my social media are lit up red, but that's normal; it's probably memes from my friends. I tap the number and squeeze my eyes shut while my DMs load, then open them.

There are messages from Talia and Kev, a couple replies from randoms at school and girls on the basketball teams, and—

One from Mel.

Oh my god.

I open it. The time stamp on the message is from just a few minutes ago.

Yesterday was rly fun, she wrote. What u up to today?

Just woke up, heading to bball practice soon, I say. How about you?

I hit send before I remember to analyze it. But that's a pretty good message. Casual but conversational.

I don't have much time to overthink before her reply pops up: Nice! My day is pretty chill. Hangin with a friend later.

I squeal and hug the phone to my chest. Maybe she's lying in bed right now, too. Maybe I was the first thing she thought of. I wonder what her room looks like, if it's small or big, what color the walls are, what kinds of posters she has up.

My phone pings, and I look at the message. It's a picture of the cutest dog I've ever seen, a golden pit bull puppy with its tongue hanging out, gazing up at the camera.

Midas is ready for his breakfast, Mel writes.

OMG he's SO CUTE! That's a perfect name. How old is he?

Three months old, she says. My dad's friend's dog had puppies!

Amazing!

Hope you get to meet him soon ;)

I shriek and throw the phone down. She wants me to meet him? SHE SENT A WINKY FACE EMOJI?

I screenshot the message and text it to Talia. So this just happened.

O M F G, she says, each letter in its own message, with a line of emojis to follow it: double exclamations, levitating man, screaming face, heart eyes, puppy face.

I reopen the message with Mel. I'd love that, I say, with a halo emoji.

I gather my stuff in a daze and float downstairs to grab a snack bar before heading out.

Is this my life? I not only met a cute girl, but she's flirting with me, too?

It's finally happening. I can't believe I was so frustrated a few days ago. I know it's only been a day, but I'm feeling really good about Mel. About . . . us?

There's not an us yet.

But if this keeps up . . .

Maybe there will be.

We DM back and forth the whole rest of the day, sending each other videos, memes, and pics of what we're doing. I learn she's the youngest of five siblings, her dad is a pastor, her mom is a teacher, and she's a huge fan of Lizzo. (Which, same.)

We're still going strong on Friday, and during practice, I make Mariah take a video of me sinking a three pointer from the top of the key.

After practice, I send Mel the video before I can stop myself. This one's for you, I say. It's the boldest thing I've ever said to a crush—which isn't saying much, since I don't usually talk to my crushes. But still. Sending it lights up my body with adrenaline, and the wait for a response is agonizing. The minutes tick by as I stand at my bus stop staring at the thread.

But it doesn't take long.

Basketball QUEEN! She replies, with a crown emoji and a heart eyes emoji.

Oh my god. Hearts have entered the chat.

I send an emoji blowing a kiss. *Am I . . . flirting back?*
And doing it pretty well?
I don't know who this Hayley is, but I like being her.
So . . . when do I get to see you again? she says.
My whole body warms, and I grin down at my phone.
When are you free? I ask.

On Sunday morning, I'm up early, my body buzzing with crush energy. It's never felt like this before, though. Nobody's ever liked me back. And I didn't even have to make the first move.

When I come into the kitchen, Dad is at the stove tending the sizzling hash browns, and Sam is mixing the batter, the waffle maker plugged in and warming on the counter beside her. She looks up and her eyebrows almost fly off her head.

"Who are you and what have you done with Hayley?" she shrieks.

Dad shushes her, laughing.

"I get up early sometimes," I say.

She snorts. "No, you don't."

I open my mouth, then close it again. She's right. I beeline for the fridge and grab the orange juice.

"Hayley." I turn around, carton in hand. Dad's watching me with an amused look on his face. "What's up?"

"Um." I can't hold back my smile. "I met someone."

"Really?" Dad holds up a hand. "Put 'er there."

I roll my eyes, but high-five him anyway, and go pour myself a glass of juice.

"So tell us about her," Dad says. "They? What's this kid's pronouns?"

"She/her," I say, and launch into the story, beginning with the moment Jacob pointed her out to me in the pool. When I get to the part where Mel asked for my social, Dad fist-pumps.

"Way to go, Mel," he says. "Wow, you kids have so much more confidence than I did at your age."

I shrug. "I guess."

"So, do you have a date?"

"Well . . ." I pull my phone out of my hoodie pocket and open our DMs. There it is: the time Mel can meet up. "We're hanging out Wednesday at two."

"Where?"

"Caffe Vita on the Hill."

"You'll text us when you get there and when you leave, right?"

"Dad, it's fine."

"Look, I trust you, kid, but I don't know her. Safety first."

I sigh. "OK, I will."

"Wow, you're up early," Mom says, coming into the kitchen.

"Hayley got a date," Sam says.

"Sam!" I glare at her.

"What?"

"It's *my* news."

Sam shrugs.

I make a face at her and tell the whole story again. Mom

listens raptly. "That is a meet-cute if I've ever heard one," she says when I finish.

"I know, right?" I smile. "She's really cool. I can't wait for you all to meet her. I think she's going to get along with my friends really well, too. And if Talia dates her person—"

"Talia got a date, too?" Dad exclaims.

So then I have to tell the whole story of the salon and the summer love strategy—because even though Mom has told Dad, Sam doesn't know about it—and by that time, breakfast is ready. I finish telling them everything just as Ella shuffles in, hair a mess.

"Why are you all so excited?" she mumbles, sliding into the open seat at the table.

Dad and Mom look at each other and laugh. Sam opens her mouth but this time, I beat her to it.

"I have a date!"

Ella nods. "Cool." She takes the plate Dad hands her.

"Do you want to hear the story?" I ask.

She just shakes her head.

"Thank god," Sam says. "Can we please eat?"

I huff, but it's short-lived. The waffles smell too good, and Dad brings out his homemade strawberry compote, and all I can focus on is breakfast.

Mostly.

I can feel my phone buzz as notifications come in, and I can't help smiling.

I have a date.

Caffe Vita sits on Pike Street in Capitol Hill, in the square of blocks that form the core of the neighborhood. The whole area has this midsummer glaze, the sun beating down from the clear blue sky, the businesses teeming with people out to enjoy the warm weather. Pride flags for all the different letters of the gay alphabet hang in every window I pass.

The coffee shop is sandwiched between a few other small businesses. There are a few tiny bistro tables out front, and there she is as I walk up that afternoon: Mel, a grin lighting up her round face.

"Hey there," she says, standing up to greet me.

"Hi." I giggle. I'm nervous.

She smiles. I smile. She sticks her hands in her pockets. "So, you wanna . . ." she jerks her head at the door.

"Yes. Definitely."

She holds the door for me—this is not a drill, SHE HOLDS THE DOOR FOR ME!—and I walk into the cozy, cool interior of Caffe Vita. Everything is dark wood, the north-facing windows keeping it dimly lit. Soft indie pop music plays on the sound system.

"What can I get for ya?" The barista looks between us.

"I'll have an iced chai," I say, and look over at Mel. "What about you?"

"No, no." She waves a hand and pulls out a wallet. "I've got this."

Oh my god.

This is, like, a real date.

"Are you sure?"

She nods. "Of course." She places her order for a vanilla Italian soda. Classy.

Once she's paid, I go outside to grab a table while she waits for our drinks (another thing she volunteers to do. Swoon).

She joins me and we both sip our drinks and then start talking at the same time. We stop and laugh.

"You first," she says.

So I answer her question: how was my day? She laughs when I tell her I got home from practice with only an hour to spare before our date.

"I'm impressed," she says. "It took me that long to figure out which sneakers to wear today."

"How many sneakers do you have?" I ask.

"Ten pairs so far." She grins at my wide-eyed look. "I'm kind of a sneaker head."

"I can see that."

"I work at Starbucks, and whatever I don't use to help the fam, I spend on me. I save some of it, and the rest . . ." She gestures at her perfectly white Adidas.

"Wow. That's really cool." I like that her family is so important to her. And she already has a job? I feel a little self-conscious; I could work if I wanted to, but I don't have to, and I know that's a privilege. *Maybe I should have paid. But she offered.*

"I also get to treat pretty girls," she says as if she read my mind.

I feel the blush instantly.

"Aw, cute! You are so red." She laughs.

"*You* are so confident," I blurt out before I can stop myself.

She rubs a hand over the back of her head, wrinkling her nose. "Is it too much?"

"No. It's just . . ." I fiddle with my cup. "I just don't have that at all. I've never . . . This is my first date." Oh no. I didn't want to say that; my words are going faster than my filter, like usual.

"Ever?" Her eyebrows raise.

I'm cringing inside. *Could I be any more awkward? It's too late now, though.* "Yeah."

She puts a hand over her heart. "I'm honored."

I hide my face.

"Hey, don't be embarrassed! It's cool. We all gotta start somewhere."

"When did you . . . start?" I peek at her through my fingers.

She chuckles. "Seventh grade."

"Seventh grade?!"

"Yeah, I was a li'l player."

"Were you out?"

"Oh, from jump. I always knew I liked girls."

"How was your family with it?"

"They were fine. Dad took a minute, but he came around." She shrugged. "My older brother came out around the same time, and one of my dad's friend's kids, Ronnie, had been out forever, since I was little, so that helped. What about you?"

"Well, the first person I told was my friend Talia in sixth grade. She told me she was trans pretty soon after that. And then we told our parents. It was kind of like a pact, actually." I laugh, remembering what we did. I guess it makes sense that we made another pact for finding love this summer, too. "We made this whole official document, a Certificate of Coming Out, and a presentation for each of our parents. Once we each did our presentations, we signed the certificate and had our parents sign it, too."

"Whaaat? That's so cute." Mel grins.

"Right? It was super nerve-racking at the time, more for Talia than me because my parents have gay friends, so I figured they'd probably be cool with it. Her parents do, too, but you know . . . it's different for trans people."

Mel nods. "Yeah, my cousin is trans. There's a lot of visibility now but a long way to go for acceptance. It's kind of like, trans folks are where queer folks were ten or twenty years ago. And things aren't even guaranteed good for queer folks still!"

"Totally!"

Mel takes a long drink of her soda. "How did it turn out?"

"Talia's parents definitely needed some time to absorb it, but they made an effort to educate themselves." I turn my cup around in my fingers. "Her dad said something pretty cool, actually. That he doesn't have to totally get it to love his own kid; all he has to do is listen, learn, and support her. That he's not trans, so he can't actually understand fully, but it doesn't matter."

"Wow."

"Yeah." I can still hear Talia's voice, hushed on the phone as she told me that night. "And Talia's amazing like that, too. She's just so smart, and her own person, and funny in this dry way. She's got an amazing mind. She can absorb new information really quickly, so she's super accepting and open, and she knows me . . . sometimes it feels like she knows me better than I do."

"She sees you." Mel's eyes are on me, her gaze warm and gentle.

I nod, my heart fluttering.

She leans back in her chair. "Talia sounds dope."

I smile. "Yeah. She's my best friend for life."

"Nice." Mel looks up and down the street. "It's so nice out today. You want to go for a walk?"

"I'd love to."

The air is warm, the breeze only slightly cooler. It's a perfect summer day. We weave through the tourists and families and neighborhood residents out walking their dogs, past Elliott Bay Books with their Pride display up in the front window, across to Cal Anderson Park. On our left is a set of tennis courts now used for skating and other random activities. Today there's a girl doing hula hoop tricks while music blasts from her portable speaker. To our right is a huge Astroturf field with groups of people scattered across it, picnicking and tossing Frisbees. We stroll up toward the other end of the park, past the community garden, along the walkway next to the reflecting pools. The benches along it are full of people, and so is the grass behind them. We chat about everything and nothing: her friends, my friends, school, random stories from childhood, our favorite movies, politics, and more.

"Man, I feel like I could talk to you forever, but I should head home," Mel says finally. "Which way you going?"

"I'm just walking that way," I say, pointing back in the direction we came. "I live pretty close."

"I'm taking the light rail back to Rainier Beach," she says, naming the area of South Seattle where she lives, which means she has to walk in the exact opposite direction to get to the train station. "So I'll see you soon?"

"Yeah, sounds great!"

We stand up and smile at each other. This feels like the moment you usually kiss a date, and part of me wants to, but I don't know if I'm ready to kiss her. It's only been one date.

"Can I hug you?" she asks.

My body relaxes. She's so easy to be around. I don't feel any pressure. "Yes, absolutely."

The hug is brief but warm; her arms feel strong, and she smells like spicy cologne. Then she's backing up, flashing me that peace sign again, and I wave goodbye. As I walk through the neighborhood back home, my steps feel light, like I drank a double shot Americano instead of a chai.

I pull my phone out a few blocks later. Maybe it's too soon to text her, but I don't really care. Rules are silly, and we just had a perfect date.

That was so fun, I type. Wanna do it again sometime?

CHAPTER TEN

"Wow!" Mariah says when I greet her the next morning. "Who messed up and gave you coffee?"

One of my parents' few rules is that we don't drink coffee. That doesn't stop me from getting the occasional Frappuccino, but I always regret the crash afterward way more than I enjoy the boost. I think caffeine just doesn't work with my brain. But I am feeling pretty peppy this morning.

I grin. "No coffee."

"OK . . ." Mariah squints, grabbing a ball and following me to a nearby basket to warm up. She banks a shot off the backboard through the net, runs forward, and snags the rebound. On the landing, she whips around, shoes squeaking, and points at me. "Wait a fucking minute. I know that grin. You have a new crush."

I blush and shoot a three from the top of the key. Nothing but net.

"Hayley! You better tell me."

I head over to my bag and fish out my phone. When I show her Mel's account, she nods appreciatively. "She's cute."

"Thanks." I blush, putting the phone back in my bag. "She's really cool. We had our first date yesterday."

"Nice! You gonna see her again?"

I toss Mariah the ball and run ahead of her back to the court. "That's the plan!"

She drives up behind me, pulls up for a shot, and I jump to block her, but I'm too late. She sinks it and we high-five. I'm feeling *good*.

Warm-up winds down, and once everyone's circled up, we go over the plan for the day. Sherika hangs back as I take the lead, which feels good. At first, she was running things and I assisted. But now that I'm feeling more confident, it's like she sees that and is giving me the opportunity to step up, and because of her help—her mentorship—the varsity girls are listening to me, too.

Halfway through practice, I look up and see Coach on the sidelines. She's watching us run drills, and when she sees me looking at her, she gives me a thumbs-up and a big grin. I wave back. I don't know how long she's been standing there, but I know I've been doing a good job keeping the other girls focused today.

"What did I tell you?" Mariah says as she jogs to the back of the line behind me. "You're making varsity next year for sure."

"Who's making varsity?" Trinity lines up behind Mariah.

"Hayley," Mariah says.

"You don't know that!" I say. I want it to be true, but I don't want to get too ahead of myself.

"Oh yeah, for sure," Trinity says. "That or JV captain."

"That's what I'm saying!" Mariah says.

"Only if y'all come with me." I hold out a hand.

"Deal," Mariah says, and we do our handshake.

When the drill wraps up, I look around, but Coach is gone. The rest of practice goes fast; we divide into four teams for a mini-tournament, and my team wins.

I'm gathering my stuff together, chatting with Anh and Trinity, when I hear it: a chorus of oohs echoing across the gym. I look up. Some of the varsity girls are catcalling Sherika. Trey's standing in the doorway, and he's got a massive grin on his face. Sherika waves off her friends and trots over to him, and they kiss.

I wait for the pang, but nothing comes.

They kiss longer, and then disappear out the door together. Her friends follow behind, talking among themselves.

My phone buzzes. I pull it out, but it's just Jacob texting the group chat about some show he wants us to watch. I haven't heard from Mel yet, but my chest gets warm just thinking about her.

Wait.

I think I'm over Sherika.

My stomach swoops at the thought. *Holy shit. I did it.*

Anh and Trinity say their goodbyes, and then the gym is empty. I lock up the gear closet, scan once for anything left behind, and then head outside, locking the door behind me.

I'm over Sherika. Completely.

I smile up at the blue sky. I can't wait for my next date with Mel.

I pull my phone out of my bag, half-hoping she's DM'd me in the last ten minutes since I checked. I've been glued to my phone lately, waiting for messages from her. She hasn't, but there's a text from Talia: GUESS WHO HAS A DATE!!!

I FaceTime her immediately. "YOU HAVE A DATE?" I scream when she picks up. She flinches and bursts out laughing.

"Me and Rose just made plans," she says, grinning.

"Oh my god," I say, almost tripping over part of the sidewalk where a tree root is busting through the concrete. "What did they say? What are you gonna do? How are you feeling?"

"They said, 'I'm free Friday, how about noon?' And I said, 'That sounds great.' We're going to get ice cream. I'm feeling . . ." She waves her free hand wildly.

"ICE CREAM!" I shriek. "That's so cute!"

Her cheeks turn pink. "I know. Plus, it's low-key. So I can just get to know them better."

"Now we *have* to do a double date! You and Rose with me and Mel!" I'd called Talia as soon as I got home from seeing Mel yesterday and told her all the details.

"We should probably go on more than one date with them before we do that," Talia says.

"Taliaaaaaaa!"

"Whaaaaat?"

"I know you are the queen of planning, and I love you for it, but just fantasize with me for a second. Wouldn't it be so cute if that happened?"

"Yeah." She smiles. "It would be really cute."

"*Thank* you." I'm at the bus stop, and I look up from the phone to see the bus coming. "I gotta go, I don't wanna be that person on the bus, but I'm so excited for you and I want to hear all about it when you get home tomorrow, OK?"

She gives me a thumbs-up, I blow her a kiss, and we hang up.

Friday morning, I get a response from Mel: a heart reaction on a meme I sent her after my other message, but no answer to when she wants to see me again.

Maybe she's busy or something.

I distract myself by texting Talia to hype her up for her date.

At the end of practice, Mel still hasn't said anything else, and Talia's on her date, so I can't text her for advice on what to do. Not that I need it. Everything's fine. Not everyone is a constant texter. I just need to chill. Mel will get in touch soon.

My phone pings, and I yank it out of my bag so fast I almost drop it. But it's just a text from the group chat. I almost put away my phone, but then I do a double take.

Karina just broke up with me :(

I stare at the message from Bri. I almost don't understand it, like it's written in another language.

How is this possible? They seemed—oh.

The pool. I guess I wasn't just projecting. The energy between them *was* off.

OMG WHAT? Nooooooo! Kev texts.

Jacob sends a bunch of sad emojis. What do you need??

Idk, Bri says. She just texted me.

SHE BROKE UP WITH YOU OVER TEXT? I say.

Yup.

I can come over, practice just got done. I turn around and start walking in the direction of Bri's house.

That would be good. Bri's a pretty flat texter in general, but usually they throw in a random emoji or two. Not now. It's just text, and the vibe is totally different. I can tell they're really upset.

Everyone else is busy, except Jacob, who says he'll be over soon, too. I walk fast, and it only takes me fifteen minutes to get to Bri's house, a huge, sunset-orange old house sitting in the neighborhood near Ravenna Park. As I arrive at the bottom of their front steps, Jacob rounds the corner.

"I can't believe this is happening," he says when he gets to me. "I thought they were solid."

"I know." We head up the concrete steps, painted a teal that contrasts beautifully with the color of the house. At the top, I grab the hidden key from under the flowerpot and let us in.

The inside of Bri's house is as brightly colored as the out-side; every wall is a gallery of paintings and photographs. One of Bri's moms is an artist, and she's always collaborating with local arts initiatives or exhibiting paintings in museums around the country. She does huge paintings, mostly of Black women, in this maximalist rainbow palette. Bri's other mom is a tenured professor at the university. Neither of them are home right now, though; the house is quiet when we walk in. If Artist Mom was here, music would be blasting from the back of the house where her studio space is. If Professor Mom was here, she'd be grading papers on the couch.

We head up the stairs to the second floor. I call Bri's name so they aren't startled, and tap gently on their bedroom door.

They open it. I can tell they've been crying, and as soon as they see us, the tears well up all over again.

"Do you want a hug?" I ask.

They nod, and I wrap my arms around them while Jacob squeezes their arm and makes sympathetic noises. After a moment, Bri sighs. "Can you squeeze tighter?"

I do. When Bri wants touch, pressure helps them regulate. Once I feel them start to shift, I let go and then we settle in our usual spots—them on their bed, me in the beanbag chair, Jacob sprawled on the floor.

"I'm so sorry," I say.

"What happened?" Jacob asks. "If you want to talk about it. It's OK if you don't."

"No, I do." Bri wipes a hand over their cheek. "Um . . . well . . . we had this whole, uh, talk like a week ago. She said she wanted me to be more romantic. The thing is, I thought I was. I bring her little things that remind me of her all the time, like cool rocks I find at the park, or the candy she likes when I'm at the corner store." They pick at the bedspread, a tear rolling down their face. "And I made her an entire playlist of all the songs I was listening to when we first started getting to know each other. She liked some of the songs, but didn't understand why I put others on there, and I tried explaining that they all remind me of her because I was listening to them at the time, but she didn't really get it . . . So I've been trying to think of ways to be more romantic, but I don't know how and she didn't tell me. And I know I should just know. But I don't."

"But she understands that planning stuff isn't really your thing, right?" I think back to what Bri told us at the lake, how Karina had orchestrated a special day full of all their favorite things.

"I thought so." Bri shrugged. "I told her early on I tend to get stuck on doing the same things. And that I haven't had a girlfriend before, and I don't really understand the purpose of all that stereotypical romantic stuff. But in our talk . . ." They choke up. "She said she thought it would change once we were together for a while."

"Wow," Jacob says. "And she didn't really even give you a chance to try."

"I mean, it's OK." Bri sniffles. "She doesn't have to. I should just get it."

"No." I shake my head. "You two have been together for like, what, six months?"

"Four."

"Still. You're not some random hookup; you had a whole-ass relationship!"

"Yeah." Bri straightens up. "We were girlfriends."

"Exactly!" I throw out my hands. "You deserve a chance to make things right. Or at least an in-person breakup."

"What did she say?" Jacob asks.

"She just said she felt like things weren't working and said we should break up," Bri says.

Jacob and I make a shocked noise at the same time. We all sit together in silence.

Bri plays with one of their fidget toys. "What if I'm ..." They swallow. We wait. "What if I'm just ... not good at relationships? If I can't do basic stuff like romance—"

"Bri, no," Jacob says. "You can do romance. You just have a different idea of what's romantic than Karina does, and it's sad that she can't see that."

"Everyone has a different way that they like to be loved though, right?" Bri says. "You have to find out what makes your person feel good and do that. Like the whole love languages thing."

"OK, first of all, that guy is a homophobic Evangelical Christian with zero therapeutic training," Jacob says. His special interest is relationships and communication, and I can tell he's starting to get warmed up talking about this. "But regardless, you also have to appreciate the way the other person naturally shows their love, too."

"Exactly," I say. I think of some of the therapists I follow on socials and their videos about healthy relationships. "You showed your feelings in the way that was natural for you, and just because Karina couldn't see or appreciate that doesn't mean you're bad at relationships. Did she ever even tell you what would make her feel good? Beyond just, like, 'romance'?"

"No."

"Did you ask?"

". . . No."

"Huh." I rub the back of my hair, thinking. "Well, still. I mean, maybe you could have asked, but she also could have told you what she meant."

"Ugh." Bri buries their face in their hands. "I am so bad at communicating!"

I look at Jacob and grimace. Clearly, I'm not helping. He takes the cue.

"You can get better at that," he says.

"It's too late now." Bri says, voice muffled.

"Are you sure?" he asks.

"She said it was over. I don't want to push her."

"What did she say—like, word for word?"

Bri hands their phone over, and Jacob reads the text exchange. Then he rereads it, brow furrowing. "Oh man. Bri. She didn't say you should break up." He reads the text aloud. "'I feel like things have been weird between us lately. It seems like things aren't working. I'm not sure what to do. Should we break up?'" He puts the phone down and we lock eyes. His gaze shifts to Bri. "She's not *telling* you. She's asking. She wanted to have a conversation."

I look at Bri. They're frowning, and I can see the calculations happening behind their eyes. "So . . . I could say I don't want to break up? And that would be OK?"

"Yeah! She asked you a question. It wasn't a statement."

"This is your chance to be honest with her," I say. "You can explain that you don't know what romance means to her, and tell her about the ways you show your feelings."

"I mean, I tried to do that with the playlist, and she didn't really get it."

"Bri . . ." I trail off. Something is coming to my mind. "Did you ever tell her you think you're probably autistic?"

There's a long silence. Then Bri lets out a heavy sigh. "No."

"Do you think that might help her understand about the ways you show you like her?" I ask. "I know you said you tried to tell her and she didn't get it. Maybe she would if she understood more about what it means to be neurodivergent. If you sent her some of those accounts you follow."

"But I'm not officially diagnosed. What if she doesn't believe me?"

"Well, you won't know unless you find out," Jacob says. "And if she doesn't believe you, then that says more about her than you."

Bri groans, smushing their hands against their face. "This is so uncomfortable."

"Yeah," I say. "But you like her, and she likes you, and it seems like she wants to talk, so the door is already open. You just have to walk through it. She wouldn't have asked you if she just wanted to go straight to break up."

"I guess."

"Bri."

"OK, OK."

"Can I ask you something else?" I watch them, and they nod. "Why didn't you talk to us earlier? Like when you were first starting to worry?"

They pick at the comforter. "I don't know . . . everyone just seemed so happy. I didn't want to bring you all down."

"Bri." I smack my forehead. "It doesn't bring me down when you're having problems! I don't want you to be sad, obviously, and it makes me sad to see you sad, but it doesn't ruin my life or anything."

"Seriously," Jacob adds. "Next time, tell us when you're struggling. We're your friends. We love you."

"Thanks." Bri's eyes fill with tears again. "Can I have another hug?"

"Absolutely." I jump up and sit down beside them, wrapping them in my arms. When we pull back from the hug, Jacob is standing there holding out Bri's phone. They take it from him.

"You do you, but I think you should text Karina about this," he says.

They nod and take a deep breath, opening the message thread. "Tell me what to say, Communication King."

After dinner that night, I curl up in my nest of blankets to watch some cartoons. Talia promised to FaceTime me once I was free, but she's still eating with her parents, so I have to wait for the details on her date.

My mind is still on Bri. After they texted Karina, Jacob and I stuck around for a while to distract them. They drew both of us while we played video games, and eventually Karina texted back. She was relieved and wanted to meet up and talk things out with Bri, but I still feel buzzy from their almost-breakup. It's not my relationship, obviously, but I love them together. It was the first relationship any of my friends have had, and it gave me hope for my own future relationship.

My phone vibrates.

"Finally!" I say when I pick up.

Talia grins. "Were you just wasting away waiting for me?"

I throw a hand to my forehead and pretend to faint back onto my pillow. "I'm weak! I require an infusion of romance immediately."

"But of course!" She settles back onto her own bed, pulling her weighted blanket over her chest. "So. I know I sent you pics of my outfit before I left."

I nod. It was a super-cute, classic Talia look: A white T-shirt tucked into high-waisted shorts, with a wrist full of bracelets for a low-key fidget toy. Her hair was up, and she was wearing small gold hoops. "You looked so cute."

"Thanks!" she says. "Rose looked really cute, too. They were wearing the vest they had on at the salon, and they dyed their hair—wait. Let me start at the beginning."

I smile. Talia always has to give me as much context as possible. Every detail is important to her. She says it's because she can't tell which details need to stay and which should be left out when telling a story, and sometimes she gets self-conscious about talking for too long, but I like the way she notices everything.

She takes me start to finish through the date: her walk down into Capitol Hill and how she was glad she put on extra deodorant because she got so sweaty; the vegan ice cream shop Rose picked and their delicious gluten-free waffle cones; the cute little bench outside where they sat and ate their ice cream as fast as they could but it still melted; how Rose went inside to get them both napkins, and then someone walking a bulldog came along and they got to pet the bulldog—I can see it like a movie in my head as she talks. Their conversation flowed really well, and Rose told them all about astrology and how it works.

"And then they walked me home, even though it was the opposite direction from their bus," Talia says. She pauses, and her face flushes.

"Oh my god. Did you kiss?"

She shakes her head. "It kind of seemed like they wanted to, though? We looked at each other for a long time, and they kept giggling, but I didn't really want to kiss them. I know that sounds weird."

"I mean, I didn't kiss Mel," I remind her.

"But you wanted to."

"Yeah."

"Yeah, see . . . I didn't want to."

"Huh." I watch her face. She's not making eye contact anymore. "Maybe you just need to get to know them more?"

"You're probably right. They are really cool." She looks at me again and smiles.

"That's awesome!" I raise my hand like I'm going to high-five her through the phone, and she mimics me. "We did it! We had our first dates."

"We did it!" She echoes, grinning, and flaps her free hand.

Then it's my turn for story time, and I tell her what happened with Bri and Karina. "It just made me think—I mean, it was such a freaky miscommunication. They could have broken up just because of the assumption Bri made about Karina's text."

Talia shakes her head. "I'd be so stoked to get the kind of gestures that Bri does for Karina. How is that not romantic enough?"

I shrug. "I don't know. Everyone's different, though."

"It just all seems so effortless from the outside," Talia says. "I mean, my parents have been married for twenty-five years and they made it work, even when they were having problems. And yours are, like, couple goals."

"I know." I throw up my hand. "My parents seem perfect together. And so did Bri and Karina."

"What do people do when there's a really big problem? Not that Bri and Karina's thing is trivial. But you know what I mean." Talia frowns.

"Couples' counseling, maybe? Your parents did that."

"Yeah. What if you can't afford that, though?"

We both lie in our beds in silence. *Have my parents ever had problems like Bri and Karina have? Or something even worse, and I just never knew?* I assumed they were just always good together. I assumed all you needed to do was find your person and then things would fall into place. Easy, like in the movies.

I've been fantasizing about having someone to date for years, but now it feels like I made up movie scenes for my life without thinking about the characters. I've spent so much time thinking about this mystery girl and all the amazing experiences we could have together, and I made that list, but I haven't even factored myself into the equation.

What would I be like as a girlfriend? What's it really like to be part of a couple, to have someone to go on dates with, to kiss, to hold hands?

I always assumed it would be great. But that was just my imagination. Bri and Karina are so good together, and they like each other so much, and they still almost broke up. Even with Mel—we had such a good date, and I've barely heard from her since.

"I don't know," I say finally. "This is more complicated than I thought."

CHAPTER ELEVEN

THE NEXT MORNING, I have a sick feeling in my stomach. I still haven't heard back from Mel. I sent her a song by a band I'd told her about on our date when I got home from Bri's, but she hasn't replied yet.

I think I'm getting ghosted, and it doesn't feel good.

It also doesn't make any sense. We had a great date. I scan the memory for any sign of weirdness, but there isn't anything.

The fluttery, crushy feeling is changing now. I get this nervous swoop every time I check my phone, and then a wave of disappointment when there's still nothing from her. I don't know what to do. That was my first date, and now this might be my first rejection. From someone I actually went on a date with, anyway.

I try to reason with myself, tell myself that I don't really know what's up, that something could have happened, or maybe she's really busy, or maybe she's just bad at texting. But we were texting a lot before our date.

I don't want to be weird or desperate, though, so I don't message her again.

"Hayley?"

I look up from my bowl of cereal. Mom is there in the kitchen, filling a water bottle. I was so deep in scrolling social media that I didn't even notice her come in. She looks at me with concern.

"Are you OK, honey? You were so happy a few days ago, and now you seem really low."

I sigh. I told her all about my date, and she was so excited for me. Now I have to walk it back, and that makes it feel even worse. "I think Mel's ghosting me."

"Oh, sweetie." She sets her bag down and pulls out a stool to join me at the counter. "I'm sorry. I remember that feeling."

"It's so embarrassing."

"I know," she says. "And we didn't even have smartphones to help us torture ourselves back then."

"Yeah." I lean my head on my hand. "Like, I'd rather she just told me straight up if she's not feeling it anymore. Waiting feels awful."

"I get that." Mom rubs my back. "Her lack of communication says a lot more about her, though."

I fidget with my phone, spinning it around on the countertop. "I just don't know what to do. Should I text her again?"

"You know, the finer points of modern dating etiquette are kind of beyond me, but it seems OK to me to reach out one more time and check in."

"Maybe."

"I gotta go meet up with a friend, but keep me posted, OK?" She kisses my hair. "I love you."

"I will. I love you, too."

She leaves and it's just me again, stirring my spoon slowly through the sugary milk at the bottom of my bowl. After a few minutes, I pick up my phone and compose a message.

Hey! Just checking in about hanging out again. Let me know what works for you. I reread it. Seems OK. Direct but breezy. Not like I've been obsessing over her for the past few days.

I send it before I can stop myself and then put my head down on the table. *Who knows if she'll even respond. I don't even know where things went wrong. Maybe if I—*

Ping.

I grab my phone, and there it is. A message from Mel.

Hey, I'm sorry I left you on read this long. That wasn't cool. I really liked hanging with you, but I've been talking to my ex again recently and we're gonna try again. I hope you have a cool summer though. I'm still honored to be your first date.

I close my eyes. I'm not completely shocked, but my heart feels like it's imploding right now.

I really liked Mel. I thought unrequited crushes were hard, but this is a whole different kind of hurt. There's something sweet about pining, sometimes. I can just imagine what the other person is like, and I never have to worry about them hurting me.

My nose stings, tears welling up in my eyes. It feels silly to be upset over someone I barely knew. We only had one date, and I didn't have all that much time to build her up in my head like I have with my past crushes. But still. This feels so unfair.

What does that other girl have that I don't? And what if there isn't even an ex? What if Mel is just trying to let me down easy and she just doesn't like me?

I shouldn't have told her it was my first date. I probably sounded like such a baby.

I wanted to meet her family. And her puppy. We won't go on another date. And she won't come to my games, and I won't go cheer her on at hers.

A sob catches in my throat. I set my phone down, put my head on my arms, and cry. I hate dating. I hate getting crushes.

I hate getting rejected.

I hate getting hurt.

I cry like that for a long time, until my neck starts to ache and I can't breathe through my stuffed nose. Finally, I straighten up and reach for the box of tissues nearby. I take deep, shaky breaths, tapping my chest, until I feel a little calmer. Then I pick up my phone again and open FaceTime.

"What happened?" Talia says as soon as she answers the call and sees my tearstained face.

"Mel got back with her ex."

"What?!"

"She was nice about it." I shrug and try to smile.

"Hayley. You're allowed to be sad." Her words and her kind eyes, fixed on me, get me right in the heart, and I start sniffling all over again.

"I was trying not to get too ahead of myself," I mumble. "But I really kinda thought this might be it."

"It seemed like she was really cool," Talia says.

"She was," I say, voice wobbling, and then I'm for real crying.

Talia makes sympathetic noises while I sob, until the tears subside and I open my eyes. "I'm sorry," she says. "You deserve someone cool who likes you back. You're funny, and kind, and amazingly athletic—"

"I wouldn't go that far." I laugh through my tears.

"You are! And you need to believe in yourself more," Talia says firmly. "We're having a sleepover tonight. Get your stuff and come over, OK?"

"OK," I say, rubbing my face with the back of my hand. "Thanks, Talia."

It doesn't take me long to gather what I need, and within a few minutes I'm trotting through the neighborhood to her house. It's another beautiful sunny day, but it's way hotter than normal; we're probably headed for another heat wave. I'm sweating by the time I arrive. She's standing on the porch waiting for me, and I walk straight up to her and into a long hug.

"I love you, Hayley," she says.

"I love you, too," I say into her shoulder.

Inside the house, I kick off my sandals and follow her to the kitchen, sliding into one of the spinny stools at the island in the middle.

"She did send me this really nice text about it, though, and didn't leave me hanging too long," I say, twirling around in the chair for a minute before facing forward.

"I guess that's the right thing to do." Talia rummages through the fridge. "I mean, the real right thing to do would be to keep dating you, because hellooooo!" She turns and gestures at me. "You're *you*. Her ex . . . pshhhh." She waves her hand.

I can't help but smile. "Thanks."

"No need to thank me for the truth." Talia grabs a key lime LaCroix and slides it across the island to me.

Like most houses in Seattle, she doesn't have air-conditioning. All the windows are open, but it's still uncomfortably warm, so once I finish my drink, we decide to walk down into Capitol Hill and get some ice cream. We never get tired of ice cream, even though Talia had some with Rose yesterday.

Talia's putting on her sandals when I notice. "We match," I say. I'm wearing my white Birkenstocks, and her sandals are white, too; my romper is dark purple with little flowers all over it, and she's wearing one too, except hers is lavender with a feather pattern.

"Oh my god." She laughs. "We look like one of those lesbian couples that are all coordinated."

I giggle, too. I feel lighter again, and happy, the way I always feel around Talia. Lately it feels like our friendship has been extra good. I look forward to seeing her, and I feel energized when I leave, thinking about our next hangout and the fun stuff we have planned for the summer.

Speaking of which. "The MUNA show is next week. I guess I need to go back to the strategy again," I say as we head out the door. I try to laugh again, but it's obviously half-hearted. "You've got Rose locked down, though."

Talia makes a noncommittal noise.

I look over at her. "What?"

"So . . ." She grabs a curl, pulling it through her fingers. "I don't think I want to go on a second date with them."

"Oh! Why not?"

"I'm just not really feeling it?" She shrugs. "They're really cool, and I can see us being friends, but . . . going out with them after listening to you talk about Mel, I realized that I've never really felt that way about someone I don't know well." She glances over at me. "And I've been doing some research."

I pick a leaf off a bush as we pass, rolling it up in my fingers over and over as we cross into the busier streets of the neighborhood.

"I think I might be demisexual," Talia says. "And demiromantic."

I know what that is. Where you have to have an emotional bond with someone before you feel sexually attracted to them. Demiromantic is the same, but for romantic feelings.

I crush the leaf and toss it away. "That makes sense."

"Right? I mean, I can count the crushes I've had on, like . . ." Talia puts up two fingers and laughs.

"There was Dustin in eighth grade."

"Right. When we were spending all that time together because I was tutoring him."

"And then you stopped talking about him once that was over."

"And I still didn't want to, like, make out with him or anything. I'd probably need even more time to feel that."

"Oh my god." I throw up my arms. "Talia! I'm so excited for you. That is so you. And I'm like, the opposite. Someone just blinks at me and I swoon."

"You're a liiiittle more discerning than that." Talia laughs.

"That's true. I am gay, after all."

Talia smirks at me and rolls her eyes. I stick my tongue out. It hadn't occurred to me that one of us might find someone but not want to keep dating them. It makes sense, though, whether for demi reasons or because the person isn't the right fit.

Or has an ex they're still hung up on. I massage my chest briefly, Mel's face flashing through my mind.

"So I guess we'll both be back on the hunt for the concert?" I ask.

Talia makes a face. "Tbh, I've been feeling kind of anxious about trying again. It's just, like, a lot of pressure." She looks at me sidelong. Her eyes are serious. "I was hoping we could maybe take a break for a while."

As soon as she says it, my whole body settles. I feel calm in a way I haven't felt the past few weeks. We started this to help me get over Sherika, and it worked, even if I didn't end up with a girlfriend in the process. Maybe now I can just enjoy the summer and being with my friends.

"Yeah, I'm down for that."

"So the concert's just us? Best friend time?"

I smile at her. "Sounds perfect."

We wander all over the neighborhood, finishing our ice cream—mint chocolate chip, of course—as fast as we can while it melts onto our hands. We run our hands under the water in the bathroom at Cal Anderson to wash the stickiness off. I remember walking around the park with Mel on our date, and when I get a little emotional, Talia stops, and we hug by the fountain. We circle around to the thrift stores on Broadway for a distraction and have fun trying things on, showing off to each other, finding the ugliest or weirdest clothes we can, and basking in the air-conditioning.

That's one of the things I love about Talia. It doesn't matter what we're doing, we can make it fun. Even when we're bored, we can be bored together. I never feel like I have to be different when I'm with her—I don't have to put on a social mask or pretend to enjoy things I don't. Not that I feel that with my other friends either, but Talia and I have known each other so long there's another layer of comfort there. We just get each other.

"Have you talked to Bri today?" she asks.

It's getting into the evening, and we're strolling back up into our neighborhood. People are starting to come out to hit the restaurants and bars, dressed in their summer going-out clothes.

I watch them, wondering what I'll be like when I'm older, when I can do that. *Will I want to? Will I like drinking? What will dating be like then?*

"We've texted a little," I say. "They've sent me some ideas of posts and accounts they want to share with Karina about being neurodivergent."

"That would be so nerve-racking." Talia shakes her head. "I haven't even thought about how to tell dates I'm autistic. With you all, I never have to think about it. I forget not everyone's like us."

"Neurotypicals are a mythical creature at this point. Have *you* ever met one?" I dodge around a group of chattering, laughing women in tiny dresses and follow Talia around the corner toward the more residential part of the neighborhood.

Talia laughs. "Kev is, supposedly. And I guess Karina, though she's been hanging out with all of us."

"Yeah, I don't think Bri needs to worry about if Karina will be cool. She knows you and Jacob are autistic, and she's met me."

"An ADHD queen if I've ever seen one."

I grin. "I do relate a lot to that. But I relate to being autistic, too. Who knows? My family definitely isn't typical."

"There's so much more variety to how human brains process things than we even know," Talia says, gazing up at the lush branches of the trees arcing above us. "Everything we go through, everything we are, affects how we each see the world. If we could all embrace that, the world would be better off."

"I know, right?" My phone pings. It's Bri, texting to tell me they're about to meet up with Karina and talk. I show Talia and then send them good luck vibes from both of us.

"We should invite them to join us if they want," Talia says.

I feel a flicker of something. Disappointment? *Weird*. Of course I want to be there for Bri. Talia and I hang out together one on one all the time.

"Totally." I text the invite to Bri, and they thumbs-up it.

When we get back to Talia's house, something smells amazing. Her mom looks up when we enter the kitchen. She's tiny, the opposite of Talia, who got her dad's height. "Perfect timing," she says in her New York accent. "I need one of you to watch this soup while I go give my mom a call back. She's worried about radiation from her cell phone again, so we're going to talk about that on our cell phones."

I snort and circle around to take her place at the stove.

"I think all our brains are pretty irradiated by now," Talia says. "Phones won't make much of a difference."

"Well, what're you gonna do?" Talia's mom shrugs. "I got ice cream," she calls back over her shoulder as she leaves the room.

We look at each other and face-palm. Of course.

It's not until the next morning, when I'm walking home after Talia and I make pancakes for breakfast, that it hits me. Talia put up two fingers when we were talking about how many crushes she's had. And I only know about Dustin.

I search my mind, but I can't think of a single other person.

Who was the other crush?

We tell each other everything. Why didn't she ever tell me?

Did she like one of our friends? Does she like them right now?

I get that swooping feeling in my stomach again. We've never hidden anything from each other before. Maybe I'm making a big deal out of nothing, but . . .

This feels really, really weird.

CHAPTER TWELVE

For once, instead of thinking about my own crushes, I spend the next few days thinking about someone else's.

Talia's.

I rack my brain trying to remember if she ever showed interest in someone other than Dustin. We've always told each other everything, so I *should* know, but I can't think of anyone. Then I scan my memories of all our times together with our friends. Did she ever act different with any of them? I know she and Bri hang out often, too, but Bri has Karina, and they're not polyamorous.

Although, now that Bri and Karina are struggling . . . No. That would be so unlike Talia. She'd never try to come between them like that.

By Monday afternoon, it's still bothering me. I should check on Bri anyway, and I want to ask them if they know anything about Talia's crush, so I grab my phone. I napped in my room for a bit after practice, but it's too warm now, so I roll off my bed, head downstairs, and out into the backyard to call them.

They answer my FaceTime, and I can see from where their phone is propped that they're sketching in their room.

"What are you drawing?"

Their eyes shift back and forth between their phone and the page. "A portrait."

My stomach does that swooping thing again. "Of who?"

"... Karina."

I let out a breath. "Bri! That's so cute. So you two—"

"We worked it out." Bri grins, shading in what I can see now is Karina's long, wavy dark hair. "You guys were right. She was totally understanding of me being autistic, and she didn't have a problem with it being self-diagnosed. She told me . . ." Bri pauses. "Well, I didn't ask her if I could tell other people, so I probably shouldn't say. She's not neurodivergent in that way, but she does have some other mental health stuff that she hadn't told me about before."

"Bri!" If I didn't have to hold up my phone, I'd clap right now, so I just flap my free hand instead.

"I know." Bri's grin gets bigger as they gaze down at their drawing. "I feel like we're even closer now." They look at their phone again, and I can see their eyes are sparkling.

I'm grinning so hard my cheeks hurt. "I'm so happy for you. I'm glad it all worked out so well."

They nod fast, smile matching my own. "She even apologized for not telling me what she wanted before. So we talked about that, too. She likes when I bring her little gifts, but it's confusing to her when it doesn't really have anything to do with her specifically—like the rocks, or the songs on the playlist that aren't about love. So I'm gonna be more thoughtful about also giving her little gifts that are specific to her, like her favorite candy—she liked that. And she said she loves my drawings, so . . ." Bri lifts their sketchbook, and now I can see it's not just a portrait of Karina. Bri is there beside her. It's an illustration of a cute selfie they took on a date, with a border of flowers instead of the background of the park.

"That is so amazing! If I was an emoji, I'd have heart eyes right now."

They giggle and set the drawing down.

"Speaking of like . . . romance and stuff. . ." I trail off. They keep coloring, waiting patiently for me. "I had a question. About Talia."

Bri nods as they finish the last strands of Karina's hair. I tell them about my conversation with Talia and the mysterious second crush. "Has she ever mentioned anyone to you?"

"Nope. Does it matter?" Bri eyes me curiously.

"No, I mean, I don't know—kind of? Just. We're best friends, and she never told me."

"She probably has a reason."

"I can't think of one! Why would she hide it from me?"

"Maybe she had a crush on the same person as you at some point."

". . . Oh."

Bri shrugs.

"I guess . . . yeah. That's possible."

"Or maybe she thought she told you but forgot."

"Maybe." Talia never forgets anything, though. She's usually the one reminding me about things.

"Why don't you just ask her?" Bri says. "You know. Communication!"

"I see what you did there. Throwing my own advice back at me."

"I mean, you were right," they say matter-of-factly. I laugh, and they just shrug.

When the call ends, I sit for a few minutes on our back step, watching a butterfly flit over the wildflower bed along the edge of the yard. Bri's words replay in my mind, and it sends this squiggle through my stomach. I don't want to ask Talia because I know she didn't forget. There's no way.

So why didn't she tell me?

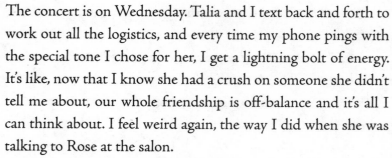

The concert is on Wednesday. Talia and I text back and forth to work out all the logistics, and every time my phone pings with the special tone I chose for her, I get a lightning bolt of energy. It's like, now that I know she had a crush on someone she didn't tell me about, our whole friendship is off-balance and it's all I can think about. I feel weird again, the way I did when she was talking to Rose at the salon.

For the first time in my life, I feel nervous about seeing her, about hanging out with her all night. I'm afraid I won't be able to hide what I'm feeling, and then she'll ask me about it, and then I'll have to either lie or tell her. Normally, I'd just ask her, but for some reason this question feels loaded. If I ask her, then I have to find out why she's been keeping it secret, and if she felt like she couldn't tell me, then maybe that means there's something really wrong with our friendship.

I'd rather just keep pretending everything's fine than risk ruining what we have.

On Tuesday night, it hits me. I text Bri frantically.

Hey you know our convo yesterday??

They take forever to respond. I nervous-scroll through social media for ten minutes until they finally text back.

About Talia?

Yeah. Could you like NOT tell her I asked about that? I don't want to make anything weird.

The minutes that go by while those three dots bounce up and down at the bottom of our message thread are excruciating.

Sure, I didn't really think anything of it, but yeah.

I let out a sigh of relief, and then Bri texts again.

So I'm guessing you didn't talk to her?

I mean what if there's something wrong in our friendship and that's why she didn't tell me?

. . . That doesn't make sense. There are way more obvious reasons than that.

It makes sense in my brain, but I don't know how to explain it to Bri.

So I just don't respond.

On Wednesday night I wait at the corner, rocking back and forth on my feet. Finally, down the block, I see Talia walking toward me, her long legs eating up the pavement.

We hug the second we reach each other, and I feel myself settle a little bit. *This is Talia. Everything's probably fine.* She seems as happy to see me as ever, a big smile on her face as we pull back.

"Happy birthday!" We chorus at the same time, and then burst out laughing.

"I can't believe we're sixteen," she says. "I feel so old."

"I know." I shake my head. I woke up this morning to a hallway lined with birthday decorations, a bundle of balloons tied to a chair at the kitchen counter, and a cupcake sitting there for me. My family never forgets birthdays, even when they're all busy. *Presents tomorrow night!* said a Post-it in Mom's handwriting stuck to the cupcake box.

"You ready to rock out?" Talia asks.

I grin. "*So* ready."

We start making our way through the neighborhood. MUNA is playing at the Paramount, a beautiful old theater just at the bottom of Capitol Hill, where it merges into downtown Seattle. The sun is getting lower, golden hour making the trees glow. Everything feels extra alive tonight, the breeze warm, the smell of cut grass and flowers surrounding us.

We come out of the residential area and cut through the Pike/Pine business district, where Mel and I met up for our one and only date. I think of her with a little pang, but not too much, which surprises me. Maybe it's because we actually went on a date and I got closure instead of pining over her for ages like my other crushes.

It does still sting that she picked someone else over me, but whatever.

Now that my hair's short, the heat is way easier to tolerate. Even so, I'm sweating by the time we're crossing over the freeway, and inside the theater isn't much better.

But it doesn't even matter because there are queer people everywhere. It feels like Pride all over again. There are so many different hair colors and pronoun pins, and everyone is smiling. The chatter of excited voices fills the lobby as Talia and I slowly wind our way through the crush of bodies.

I glance over at Talia. She's flexing and wiggling her fingers a lot, her eyes wide.

"Did you bring your earplugs?" I ask her over the din.

She digs into a pocket. A minute later, the plugs are in and she's noticeably more relaxed. I know Talia's body language by now—know when she's overwhelmed, excited, or right on the line between the two. It's always better to be safe than sorry, and when she's starting to go into sensory overload, she doesn't always remember her tools, so she's given me permission to remind her. I love being let into her world, and it makes me feel good to take care of my friends and know they trust me.

Talia slides into an eddy of space against one of the walls in the lobby and pauses there.

"Do you wanna chill here and I'll go get us something from concessions?" I ask, and she nods.

The line is less of a line and more of a swirling clump. I make my best guess about where it ends and slide in, slowly moving forward until I'm at the front. I buy us each a LaCroix and a brownie from a local chef who caters for the theater, and then I'm sliding out again, brownies in my pocket and a soda can in each hand.

Back at the wall, I hand Talia her can. "Here's to being sixteen," I say.

"And another year of friendship," she says. We clink the cans together and take a drink, and she smiles at me, her brown eyes sparkling. The peach color of her sundress complements the highlights of lighter brunette from the sun in her dark curls.

We're still smiling at each other a moment later when the theater doors open. I squeal, and Talia laughs. Grabbing my hand, she pulls me into the current of people flowing toward the general admission area at the front of the stage.

We're in the first wave, so we end up pretty close to the front. There's no seating here on the ground floor and the crowd presses in close around us. I look up to the high, ornately decorated walls and ceilings, and turn to gaze up at the mezzanine as it fills with people. It's beautiful up there, the golden railings in a curling design popping against the red seats.

Talia's still holding my hand. But it's comfortable, not weird; we don't do it a lot, but we've held hands in the past. It's nice, a physical way to show we care for each other. I squeeze her hand,

and she squeezes back. If we were scoping out cuties right now, I'd let go since I wouldn't want them to think we're dating. But we're just here to see the show, not tick off another box in the strategy, so I keep her hand in mine.

Our hands do fit really well together. Her fingers are long and slender, with rounded tips. Her hands are larger than mine, but that's not hard; my hands are smaller than most peoples'.

Bri's voice echoes in my head. *Why don't you just ask her?* My stomach flip-flops as our conversation replays in my head. I still haven't texted them back.

My hand is getting sweaty, and all the thoughts are rushing back in: *Who did Talia like? Does she still like them? Why hasn't she told me? Is there something wrong between us? No, there couldn't be, I would know; Talia's an open book, but what if . . .*

"Hayley?" Talia's voice in my ear makes me jump. I turn to look at her, and she's close enough to kiss.

Oh my god. Why did I just think that?

She's looking at me with a concerned frown. "You're totally spacing out. Everything OK?"

I open my mouth, but the house lights go down just then, and the stage lights come up and everyone's screaming. Talia turns to the stage, startled, and I let go of her hand so I can clap as the openers come on stage.

Definitely just so I can clap. Not because I'm suddenly so tingly with nerves and confusion and *something* that I feel like I'm going to explode if I keep holding her hand.

"Hello, Seattle!" The lead singer of the opening band howls into the microphone. She's a total badass, wearing bright red lipstick and a pinup-style dress, her hair in a jagged shag, tattoos up and down her arms. The band is all girls, and they rip into a fast pop-punk jam that has the whole crowd jumping and dancing. I've never heard of them, but I'm jumping up and down, too. It's fine. I'm fine. This is awesome. I love live music.

As the song winds down, I glance at Talia, and when I do I feel that *thing* again, that feeling, and all of a sudden, I know what it is. It's that rush I used to get when I saw Sherika on the court or in the halls at school. That excited-terrified-anythingispossible-wowshe'sbeautiful fizzing. And now I'm not just glancing, I'm staring at Talia as she cheers and dances wildly to the music, completely free and happy, her glasses glittering in the lights, and I know one thing for certain:

I like

Talia.

I have a crush on

Talia.

Oh my god. I have a crush on my best friend.

CHAPTER THIRTEEN

I'M CHEERING LIKE everyone else, but I can't hear a single note of the song. All I can hear is the revelation repeating in my mind:

I have a crush on Talia.

The crowd is moving and shifting, and Talia's starting to drift away from me, moving forward toward the stage. Normally I'd follow her, but instead I find an opening behind me and fight through, heart pounding, back toward the double doors. I need a breather. I need an anchor, something to hold on to before I drown in this realization.

In the bathroom, I lock myself in a stall and try to do my deep breathing exercise. Inhale for four. Hold for four. Exhale for four. Hold for four. And repeat, massaging my sternum the whole time. I haven't been to my therapist in a while; my anxiety's been easier to manage the past few years. I haven't had to use these tools as much—until recently.

I always say Talia was the first person I came out to, but really, it was my therapist. Her support helped me decide to tell someone in my regular life. And I knew exactly who that someone would be.

Talia understood the gravity of the moment as soon as I showed up to her house for our weekend hangout. When I finally got the sentence out, after a lot of pacing and false starts while she watched me patiently, she just smiled and hugged me.

"*I'm* so *happy for you,*" she said. She was almost happier than I was in that moment, and a few days later, I learned why. When I came out, it gave her the courage to tell me she was actually a girl and wanted to transition.

My anxiety got more manageable after that, especially once I told my family and no one disowned me or sent me to a conversion camp. I still don't know why I was so afraid of something like that happening. Maybe it was because I didn't see many queer people in books or movies then; maybe it was all the news items about anti-LGBTQ+ legislation; maybe it was the right-wing articles my aunt always emailed to the whole family.

I just wasn't completely sure how my parents would react.

Luckily, everything turned out fine.

I squeeze my eyes shut. Even though everything turned out fine then, it still feels nerve-racking to put myself out there. Like with Mel. I thought she liked me, but she picked her ex instead. I know I'm supposed to believe that wasn't about me. I know logically it wasn't.

But now it's Talia.

It just kind of happened. I didn't even realize I was crushing. That's never happened before; I always see a crush coming. The girl smiles and I feel a flutter. The girl talks to me and I want to hold her hand. It's easy to imagine being with people when you know you're never actually going to be with them.

I didn't see this coming.

But then it hits me: the hair salon.

The weird feeling.

I was jealous.

I was jealous of Talia liking someone else.

Someone who wasn't me.

I wanted Talia to look at *me* like that. To talk to *me* that way.

Because I had—*have*—a crush on her.

And after everything that's happened this summer—not just Mel, but Bri and Karina, and all the rejections—what if this isn't even a real crush? What if this is just me idealizing someone again, the way I always do, and it just happens to be Talia this time? I can't do that to her.

Whether my crush is real or not, I can't lose Talia.

I have to lose this crush.

I come out of the bathroom slightly calmer, though not by much. I still have to spend the whole rest of the concert with Talia. Looking at her cute face. Admiring the way her dress fits her body. Smelling her lavender body soap. *What if she tries to hold my hand again?*

My phone pings. It's a text from Talia: where are u???

Bathroom sorry!!

"Hayley?" I look up and there she is, sweaty, coming toward me into the lobby.

"I was just texting you!" My voice sounds weirdly high.

She glances at her phone. "Oh. I got worried! I looked around, and you were just gone."

"I'm sorry." Her warm, kind brown eyes—*No.* Her TO-TALLY REGULAR BROWN EYES look concerned. "The crowd was carrying you away from me, and I didn't want to fight through it."

"OK . . ." She still has that concerned look. "Just . . . text me next time or something?"

"Yeah, definitely. I'm sorry."

Then we just stand there, looking at each other. It feels like there's a hum in the air, but that might just be my ears ringing from the loud music. She snaps out of the moment first.

"I'm gonna use the bathroom, too. Wait for me?"

"You got it."

My mind is going a mile a minute while I stand there. *How do you lose a crush?* I've never made myself just *stop* liking someone. Usually it's ended when I find another crush or, like Sherika, when they start dating someone.

That's it.

I have to find someone for Talia to date.

When she comes out a few seconds later, I give her my best everything-is-normal-and-you-are-just-my-best-friend smile.

She smiles back. "Hey, I'm feeling a little overwhelmed. Is it OK if we hang back a bit to watch the rest of the show?"

"Totally."

We head into the theater and find a spot along the back wall. The floor slopes slightly upward, so the view is still pretty good. The openers are just finishing up, and the crowd is pumped.

I scan the area around us. There are a couple groups of people our age, and some of them are pretty cute. I nudge Talia. "Look over there."

She does. "What?"

"Those people are cute, right? The girl with the . . ." I scan the group quickly. "The mohawk."

"I guess?"

I glance at Talia. She's not even looking at them. I try another angle. "So what's up with Rose?"

"Rose?" She looks at me, eyebrows raised. "I decided I didn't want to go on another date with them, remember?"

"Did you tell them yet?"

"No, I . . ." She bites her bottom lip.

"Oh my god. You weren't going to *ghost* them?"

She grimaces. "I mean, we've still been talking! It's just that neither of us have talked about another date yet. I was kind of hoping it would just fade into friendship."

"Well, maybe if you got to know them, you'd catch feelings over time. Isn't that what being demi is about?"

She twists up her mouth and plays with her lower lip. She does that a lot when she's thinking, but this time it's more . . . distracting than usual.

NO. I will *not* ogle my best friend's lips.

"You should try! Just one more time. You two have so much in common. It would be so cute if it worked out." I sound fake to myself, but Talia doesn't seem to notice.

She nods slowly. "We do have a lot in common. And I really like talking to them."

"See?" I nudge her with my elbow. "Give it a shot!"

She looks over at me, her forehead crinkling, lips slightly parted. The house lights flicker and we both startle, glancing up at the stage as cheers fill the theater and people flood back onto the floor. The theater goes dark. The stage lights start to flash and change, the piped-in music stops, and the crowd roars. As the lights sweep the crowd, MUNA strides on stage: Katie to the mic, Naomi to her right, Josette to her left. I scream as they emerge, heart racing, and I hear Talia screaming, too.

They launch into the first song and I'm starstruck, eyes wide to take in as much of them as I can. Katie's red hair, shining in the spotlight, and her lilting voice belting over the beat; Josette in her white tank top dancing with her guitar; Naomi's devilish grin as she drops the beats right on top of my heart. I can't help moving, lifting my arms toward the stage. I look over at Talia and she's smiling at me wider than I've ever seen. It's like we're under a spell together, lost in the magic.

"This is amazing!" She screams over the music. Her earplugs are in, and she's stim-dancing, swaying back and forth, her fingers tapping against her thigh in time with different instruments and different parts of the beat.

"I know!" I yell back, pumping my fist in the air. I love how neither of us are too cool to freak out over this incredible band.

Gazing up at the stage, it really hits me: Talia is so much of what I want. That list I made at the beginning of the summer and more. *How did I never see this coming?*

On stage, the band moves seamlessly together and apart. I can tell how much fun they're having; how close they are. Naomi and Katie even dated for a while, a long time ago, and now they're friends. *Could I do that with someone I used to date?*

Could I do that with Talia if she liked me back and we dated and broke up?

The thought is a bolt to my heart. I can see it all in a flash: junior and senior year in bliss, holding hands at prom in matching-but-not-too-matching dresses, and then our last summer, tinged in blue sadness. Because what are the odds we go to the same college? What are the odds we make it work long-distance? I still don't know what I want to major in, much less where I'll apply.

So we'd break up. The image itself is enough to make my eyes blur with tears, and I shift away from Talia slightly, blinking fast to get rid of them. That would be the best-case scenario breakup, and how would I go back to being friends after that? How could I talk to her every day, knowing how I feel, wanting to kiss her and hold her and not being able to?

And what if it's much worse?

What if we really hurt each other and never want to talk ever again?

Katie and Naomi are the exception. I don't know how they did it, but whatever code they cracked, it isn't the norm.

I can't date Talia.

I can't even entertain the thought.

My eyes are clear now, and I turn back to her. "I'm sure!" I yell.

She tilts her head.

"You should DM Rose," I say, and she nods slowly.

I look up at the stage, at Katie sweeping her arms wide to encompass the whole crowd.

This is perfect.

Crisis averted.

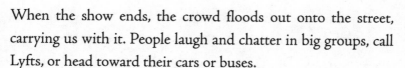

When the show ends, the crowd floods out onto the street, carrying us with it. People laugh and chatter in big groups, call Lyfts, or head toward their cars or buses.

"That was incredible," Talia says as we walk slowly back up toward the top of Capitol Hill. She's glowing, cheeks pink, sweat shining on her collarbone. I look away quickly.

"It was more than incredible. It was *iconic*," I say. "Katie's leather miniskirt?" The lead singer of MUNA is exactly the kind of queer woman I want to be when I'm an adult—powerful in her confidence, owning herself as a queer femme.

"I love her voice so much," Talia says dreamily.

"And Naomi and Josette," I say. "They are fucking *rock gods!*"

"The power stances!" Talia stops mid-stride and plants her legs, strumming an invisible guitar.

"Iconic," I repeat. "And closing the show with 'Silk Chiffon'—" I stop. It's my favorite song because it perfectly describes how it feels to crush on a girl, all shimmery and summery and bright.

It perfectly describes how it feels to be around Talia.

But she doesn't seem to notice my pause, just twirls ahead of me under the streetlight. I concentrate on my breathing as we make it to the top of the hill. This is fine. She'll DM Rose and they'll go on another date, and they'll probably catch feelings and become girlfriends. That's what I want.

"We're getting ice cream, right?" she says. Up ahead, I can see one of the ice cream shops, their windows still lit up.

"Definitely," I say. "It's tradition."

The line is out the door, and as we edge closer to the front, we stand on tiptoes to get a look at their flavors. We do this every year—I buy Talia's ice cream and she buys mine. It's completely ridiculous, because in the end we're both spending the same amount of money, but that's what I love about it. It's so us.

It's so . . .

Romantic.

I swallow hard.

"I'll have the mint chocolate chip," I tell the scooper when he comes over to help me. I look over at Talia, waiting for her to say the same.

"Can I have . . ." She stares down at the ice creams for a long moment, then smiles. "The salted caramel?"

Wait, what?

"Trying something new?" I ask, trying to keep my voice casual. I shouldn't be freaking out just because she chose a different flavor. Even though we've had the same favorite flavor for years. Even though she kept a crush a secret from me.

She shrugs, her eyes all sparkly. "Why not? I had it the other day with Rose and really liked it."

"Cool!" I say, too peppy, but she grabs our cones from the scooper and hands mine to me, and then we're moving up to the register. I pay in a daze and follow her out around the line that's now three people deep.

How did everything change in just a few days?

Having the same flavor was one of our things. Maybe it seems stupid, but now, without it, I'm realizing it was more of an anchor than I thought. Like our shared birthday and height and history.

Our everything.

I take a bite of my ice cream, but somehow, it doesn't taste the same.

 # CHAPTER FOURTEEN

T HE SUN WAKES me up in the morning. I was so tired I forgot to close the curtains when I got home. I roll over, yawning, and starfish across my bed, stretching my limbs. My feet still ache from the concert—

The concert.

Talia.

My crush.

I close my eyes again, groaning. Now that I know it's happening, I can see the signs: I want to grab my phone and see if she's posted anything new on social media. I want to come up with a reason to text her, even though I've never needed one. It's not like she's some distant, unattainable girl that I'm only connected with because we have to do a group project together.

Except she is unattainable, and I can't let myself forget that. I've only had one successful date, and it didn't go anywhere. I've never told any of my crushes that I liked them, and I'm not going to choose my crush on my *best friend* as the first one to confess. I know Talia wouldn't be mean about rejecting me, but I can't take the chance of making things weird between us. I'm not risking our friendship for the possibility of a few months or years of romance. Friendship is forever. Romance is . . .

Romance is great. What I felt with Mel on our first date alone was so much fun. But Mel wasn't my best friend.

There's too much at stake. I can't—I won't—let this feeling grow.

I take a deep breath and sit up. When I grab my phone, the number of notifications on the lock screen overwhelms me. *What happened?*

As soon as I open the first one, to the team chat, I realize what I've done.

I forgot to set an alarm when I got home from the concert, and it's twenty minutes after practice was supposed to start. There are so many notifications on my phone—*Hayley, what's your ETA? Hayley, where are you? Are you OK? We're all here . . . where are you?*

Ten missed calls. The last one is from Mariah. I'm already out of bed, packing my bag with one hand while I FaceTime her.

"Hayley! Are you OK?" Her worried face fills the screen.

"Yes! I'm so sorry, I got home late last night, and I forgot to set an alarm, and I just woke up—"

"You *just* woke up?"

I stop. Now she looks pissed. "Yeah. I'm so sorry."

"How long do you think it'll take you?"

"I mean, it depends on the bus. If I can catch the next one—"

"Hold on." She turns away from the screen and I can hear muffled talking off-screen. A moment later, she looks back at me and sighs. "Listen. I know this was a mistake, but our time might be mostly over by the time you get here, so waiting isn't really worth it. We're going to head home. Don't be late tomorrow, OK?"

"Shit. I'm sorry. I'll be on time tomorrow."

"It's cool."

"OK. Bye." I sit down heavily on my bed, all the adrenaline draining from my body.

On Friday, I set multiple alarms and arrive at the gym ten minutes early, just to be safe. Some of the varsity girls side-eye me when they come in, but mostly it seems like everything's cool. I push through the embarrassment and practice goes off without a hitch.

Normally I would have texted Talia about something like this, but now I'm second-guessing everything. Talia, of course, knows absolutely nothing about my feelings, so she texts me throughout the day like we usually do: random memes and videos, pictures of her food, and whatever she's doing at the moment. I don't know what to do. If I act normal, I risk feeding my crush even more with every text, every laugh reaction, every interaction between us. If I pull back, I risk tipping her off that something's going on.

I definitely don't want her to figure this out, so I steel myself and send replies: a few memes, responses to her messages, and a picture of the yellow roses that finally bloomed on the last unblossomed bush in our backyard.

As soon as I send the picture of the rose, I panic. Roses are symbols of love. Of romance. I shouldn't have sent her that. She might think it means something it doesn't. Even though it does. But I don't want her to know it does. *Shit.*

I look up rose meanings and the internet tells me that yellow stands for friendship. *I'm safe.*

I'm usually anxious when I have a crush, but it's more of an excited anxiety, possibilities ping-ponging around my mind and all I have to do is grab hold of one of them. This version of anxiety has me on edge in a bad way. So many of the possibilities I can see end in heartbreak and disaster for our entire friend group, not just me. I silence my phone notifications for the first time in my memory because the pings make my stomach lurch. I try to remind myself this is only day three of knowing about my crush. It will subside eventually. It has to.

By that evening, though, I'm a wreck. I started panic-baking halfway through the afternoon just to distract myself from checking my phone over and over, and when Mom gets home and walks into the kitchen, she stops dead.

"Wow." She surveys the damage, a bag of groceries balanced on her hip.

I grimace. My apron is covered in flour and so are the counters. Baking tins and sheets are everywhere—some with finished cookies and muffins, some waiting for the next batch of whatever I've concocted in my frenzy.

"So, honey . . ." She stacks one empty tin on top of another. They're both greased already, but I don't stop her, and she gingerly sets the grocery bag down in the newly cleared spot. "How are you doing?"

"I'm fine!"

She arches an eyebrow at me. I turn away, busying myself with rolling the chocolate chip cookie dough into balls and placing it on a baking sheet.

"Does it have anything to do with your summer romance scheme?"

"Summer love strategy."

"Summer love strategy. Yes. I know things didn't work out with Mel."

"I . . ." I heave a heavy sigh. If I tell one person, it'll be that much harder to keep it a secret from Talia. "I don't want to talk about it."

I hear the bag rustle and the fridge door open behind me as she starts to put the groceries away. "I'm not going to push you to tell me anything," she says. "But if it's serious, I hope you know you can come to me."

"I know."

"OK."

I can feel her standing behind me, waiting, and I swallow hard to keep the rising tears at bay. "I'll be done soon and clean up."

"No rush. I was thinking we'd order pizza with the movie tonight, anyway. Family Fun Friday, remember?"

"Oh, right." I turn around, the tears locked away for now.

"Maybe we can all enjoy the fruits of your labor for dessert." She gestures around the counters. "What did you make today? I haven't seen you bake like this since you had that big presentation in English class last year."

I point to each one in turn. "Blueberry muffins, snickerdoodles, a cheesecake that didn't really turn out, and now I'm working on chocolate chip cookies."

"You really got your dad's cooking genes."

"I guess." Mom is looking at me, and the silence stretches a little bit longer. I shift my weight from foot to foot and glance down at the cookie dough.

"OK, honey," she says. "I'm going to go upstairs and relax for a bit. Come find me if you want to talk."

I nod and give her as much of a smile as I can muster.

Her eyes search my face for a moment and then she heads out of the kitchen. I turn back to the sheet of cookies and take a deep breath. One by one, I squash them all flat.

"Movie night! Movie night! Movie night!" I can hear Sam chanting in the living room as I swipe a rag over the last crumbs on the counter.

I did a pretty good job cleaning up; you can hardly tell the whole place looked like a flour hurricane an hour ago. My thoughts are little more than a pleasant background hum. The energy of baking soaked up all the buzzy anxiety, exactly like I hoped it would. I reach for my phone on the counter, then pause. And instead of checking my texts, I just slide it into my pocket. The move feels almost impossible. It takes everything in me not to pull the phone back out to see if Talia's texted. The last meme I sent her was hilarious, and I wonder if it made her laugh. Talia has a bunch of different laughs, but my favorite is the surprised giggle she lets out when a meme really gets her.

Oh no.

I should not be thinking about her laugh.

I imagine the thought is a leaf on a stream—another tool my therapist taught me for anxiety—and let it float away.

When I make my way to the living room, the prints that usually hang on the wall opposite the front windows—photos of the bassist from the Clash smashing his guitar, Johnny Cash flipping off the camera, and Jimi Hendrix setting his guitar on fire—have been taken down and set in the corner. Dad is setting up the projector screen in the blank space so that it'll sit neatly between the two tall bookshelves. He's a film buff—though he still won't let us watch most of his favorite movies. Apparently they're too violent and obscure, and he thinks we won't like them, but whatever.

Sam and Ella are breathing hard and bickering as they move the seating into place. The couch under the front windows stays where it is, but the love seat against the wall needs to be moved back and turned around to face the screen.

"It's so heavy," Ella groans, dragging at one end of the love seat. "Hayley, come on!"

"I just cleaned up the whole kitchen. I'm tired." I flop down on the couch. Ella snorts in disgust, but neither of them argues with me.

As soon as the love seat is in place, the doorbell rings. Sam shrieks and runs to the front door to answer it.

"Thank you!" she chirps, and a moment later her arms are piled high with three large pizza boxes. She brings them to the dining room table and sets them side by side and open, the warm, bready smell drifting through the room.

My stomach growls. No, it roars. I suddenly realize I haven't eaten since I started baking—besides bites of raw cookie dough—so I pile four slices onto my plate.

"Leave some for your humble servants," Dad calls as he goes upstairs to get Mom.

Sam and Ella take the love seat, and I sit behind them on the left-hand side of the couch. The room is filled with the sound of chewing and the faint hum of the projector overhead. Mom and Dad join us, and we shuffle through the lineup of movies in our queue.

Finally, we settle on *The Breakfast Club*. The cover image has five teenagers gazing at us, and Mom and Dad say it was a hit when they were our age.

"I must have gone to the theater ten times to see it," Mom says. "It was one of the first movies that felt like it really *got* me."

As the movie begins, I feel my phone vibrate in my pocket and pull it out. Normally, our parents make us put phones away during movie night, but they're totally enthralled as the opening scenes unfold.

Soooooo guess who has a second date with Rose on Tuesday, Talia says, adding a smiley face with a halo emoji at the end.

I'm flooded with adrenaline, and I can't tell where it's coming from: excitement that Talia texted me, anxiety about my crush on her, happiness for her date, longing to be the one she's going out with—

OMG YAY, I write back, ignoring every other feeling.

No matter what, I want Talia to be happy, so I'm just going to focus on that.

I'm so caught up in my feelings about the Talia situation that I almost run straight into Sam as she comes out of the bathroom Tuesday morning. I catch a glimpse of her face, streaked with tears, as she scoots past me toward her room.

"Sam!" I turn, but she doesn't stop, and a moment later her bedroom door shuts behind her.

I can't remember the last time I saw Sam cry; she's always been pretty happy-go-lucky. Even her version of thirteen-year-old moodiness hasn't even been that moody. She's a "straight shooter" as Dad likes to say, his euphemism for "blunt to the point of rudeness."

I walk over and tap lightly on her door.

"I'm fine!" she says. I frown. Sam has never shut me out like this before, and it stings.

"It's obvious you're not," I call back.

Her door swings open and I brace myself, but she just glares at me and rushes past, backpack in hand. "I have to go to camp."

"This is the last week, right?" I follow her down the stairs, but she doesn't answer, just lets the front door slam behind her.

The thump echoes into the empty house. Mom, Dad, and Ella are already at work. I stand there, watching dust motes swirl in the air displaced by Sam's departure, mentally scanning our previous interactions. She seemed OK at movie night on Friday: excited, hungry, bursting with opinions about some of the problematic moments in the film. At the end of our post-movie discussion, she was subdued, but I thought she was just tired. She was crankier than usual at family brunch on Sunday, though. One-word answers, staring at her plate, barely even bothering to roll her eyes even when she normally would have. I didn't see her most of yesterday because she was gone by the time I woke up and went over to a friend's house for dinner.

And now the tears.

I text Ella. Sam was crying this morning. She wouldn't talk to me. Do you know what's up? I stare at the thread for a moment, then put my phone in my pocket. Ella is fanatically responsible, so I doubt she's checking her phone at work.

But a moment later, as I'm pouring my cereal, my phone buzzes. When I look at the screen, it's not Ella.

It's Talia.

Please come over. I need help.

CHAPTER FIFTEEN

I FaceTime Talia immediately.

She picks up after one ring. "Hey."

"Are you OK?"

"Yes?" Her eyebrows knit together.

"You said you needed help?"

"I do. With my outfit. My date is today."

"Oh!" I slap my hand against my face, relief washing through me. "Jesus Christ, Talia, I thought you were in trouble, like someone had broken in or you hurt yourself."

"Why would you . . ." She taps the screen, and her eyes move. "Ah. I see."

"I cannot believe you texted me that as an opening line." I scarf down cereal as fast as I can without getting sloppy. *Apparently, I care how I eat in front of her now. When did that happen?* My chest tightens.

"Well, don't worry," she says dryly. "The only thing in crisis right now is my confidence."

I want to say something, hype her up, but everything that comes to mind suddenly sounds transparently romantic: *You're so gorgeous! Anyone would be lucky to go on a date with you! Everything you wear looks incredible!* "I'm sorry! I wish I could come over right now, but I have practice and I don't want to be late again." I sound so stiff. Ugh. *Act normal, Hayley.* I get up, put the bowl in the sink, and rush upstairs to grab my basketball bag.

"Oh, right. Wait. Late again? Aren't you the keyholder?"

"Yeah." I grab the bag, sling it over my shoulder, and hustle out of the room. "I overslept the day after the concert and the whole team was waiting for me and had to cancel."

"Yikes."

"Yeah. Mariah said no one mentioned it to Coach, but . . . I just don't want to mess up again. I want to make varsity, so I need to show her I can handle responsibility." I'm outside now, jogging down to the corner to my bus stop. "I could come over after, though? What time is your date?"

"Not till later. We're meeting up at five."

"Great. I'll see you at one." At my stop, I scan the street and see I'm on time; my bus is just down the street. "I gotta go. Don't panic."

"I'll do my best." She grimaces and hangs up.

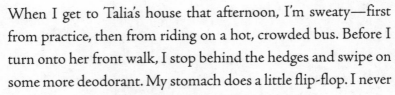

When I get to Talia's house that afternoon, I'm sweaty—first from practice, then from riding on a hot, crowded bus. Before I turn onto her front walk, I stop behind the hedges and swipe on some more deodorant. My stomach does a little flip-flop. I never used to care about how I smelled around Talia, but . . .

Whatever. I'm not going to overthink it.

Talia swings open the door moments after I ring the doorbell. "At last, my savior is here!"

"At your service." I spread my arms and do a little bow.

I follow her through the living room and toward the back of the house where her room is. When she opens the door, I see her closet is completely empty—and then I see her clothes, scattered over every surface. It's a pure tornado of anxiety.

"Having trouble picking an outfit?" I smirk at her.

"No, I just missed your room," she deadpans.

"I mean, I can't blame you. I miss my room whenever I leave it, too." I pick my way across the floor toward the bed.

"I think you just miss your bed."

"Hey!" I throw her a sassy glare. "I do spend *some* time outside of the comfort of my boudoir."

She raises an eyebrow as I sit on her bed. "Like when you're in my bed?" A jolt goes through my chest, and her eyes widen at the same time. "I did *not* mean that the way it sounded!"

"You're good!" I force a laugh and it comes out high-pitched, more like a cackle.

Talia's bright red. I'm pretty sure we were just flirting. It was so easy; I didn't even notice we'd slipped into it.

I stand back up. *Gotta get off Talia's bed. Can't think about all the times we've laid here, so close together, talking about my crushes, her special interests, school, whether God actually exists, what love might feel like—*

Shut up, brain.

"So, your outfit!" I grab the nearest shirt. "What about this?"

She wrinkles her nose, the blush fading. She's so cute when she makes that expression.

"Or this?!" I grab another shirt. It's a cute, silky button-up with a watermelon print all over it.

"Actually . . ." She steps forward and takes it. "That's cute. I forgot I had that."

"You have so many clothes. I didn't realize that." I look around.

"Yeah." She sighs. "Half of it is stuff my mom buys me from the juniors department in whatever store she happens to be shopping in. I think she's trying to be an ally, but . . . I want to look like myself, not her mini-me." She points to the first shirt I grabbed. "That's one of her picks."

I look at it. It's a powder blue cotton blouse with puffed sleeves. "It's very . . ."

"Boring? The ugliest color ever?"

"Yeah, that."

"I'm sure someone would love it, but not me." She drapes the watermelon blouse over her shoulder and rummages around. "What about this? Over the shirt?" She holds up a pair of denim overalls. "I've been meaning to cut the legs on these into shorts."

"Oh my god, yes!" I clap my hands. "With . . ." I scan the room and spot the accessory I'm looking for: Talia's light-pink baseball cap that has BOY PROBLEMS embroidered in white letters. She's a huge fan of Carly Rae Jepsen.

"That's *perfect*." She sets the clothes on her desk and looks around. "Would you help me put all this away?"

She grimaces at me, and this time when I laugh, it's real.

Once Talia's clothes are back where they're supposed to be, I head home so she can focus on getting ready for her date. It's a beautiful day out—mid seventies, with a perfect balmy breeze—but the pangs in my heart crackle like ice on the surface of a lake. In a few hours, Talia will be at Cal Anderson Park with Rose, sitting on a blanket, with a picnic of snacks and LaCroix. They'll probably talk about astronomy, and whatever else they've been DM'ing about since the concert, and at some point . . .

I swallow, pushing away the mental image of Talia kissing Rose. Maybe it won't happen today. Maybe their emotional connection isn't strong enough yet.

This is the most confusing thing to ever happen to me. I want Talia to be happy, so I want her to have a great date—but also, the thought of her being on the date . . .

It hurts. I know that polyamory is a thing, but I haven't even dated *one* person yet. I'm not ready to date multiple or know if I'd want to do that. Maybe it would be different if Talia even liked me back, but that's not my reality.

This is my reality, and it sucks. Talia's unintentional innuendo keeps popping into my head, and every time I get this squiggly feeling in my stomach. *What would it be like to kiss Talia? To actually be in her bed in a romantic way?*

It's not like I haven't noticed Talia's lips before. They're thin, with the tiniest, sweetest cupid's bow, the bottom lip slightly bigger than the top. They turn up slightly at the corners, so she always looks like she's smiling. She said it helps her mask in social situations when she doesn't want people to know she's autistic.

Wow.

If I've paid this much attention to her lips, it's possible I've had this crush longer than I realized. I just never noticed, because . . .

Because neither of us were ever in a position to actually date someone? Because it was easier to identify crush feelings on people I didn't know? Because it was less intimidating to like people who I knew deep down would probably never like me back?

Well, it doesn't matter now. Talia has Rose. Rose seems great, and if Talia's happy, that's all I want.

I turn onto my street. Usually when I leave my hangouts with Talia, I feel great, but today I just feel heavy. Once I'm on my porch, I stand there for a second, then sigh and unlock the door. Inside, it's quiet. Everyone is gone for the day. It's so nice outside, and normally I might text my friends and see if anyone wants to hit the lake.

Right now, though, my bed sounds like a great place to be. I head upstairs. I'll just lie down for a little bit. Maybe it'll help me feel better.

A few hours later, I wake up with my phone on my face and evening sunlight turning the trees outside into gold. The phone falls to the bed with a light thump as I sit up, blinking at my room. I'm groggy and too warm, and most of all, thirsty.

I stand up slowly and stretch, coming back to my body, then grab my phone and head downstairs. In the kitchen, I fill a glass of water and sip it while I check my texts.

I see Ella's first. Yeah I thought Sam seemed off the past few days. I can't remember the last time I saw her cry.

Should we talk to her? I text back.

The ellipses pop up. Yeah. I'm on the bus home, are you around?

Yup.

Ok cool. Maybe we can strategize when I get there. Is she back from camp yet?

No . . . she usually is by now.

There's a pause in Ella's responses and then: I checked the family chat—she's at a friend's tonight. See you soon.

I'm behind on that thread, so I scroll through, and there it is: an exchange between Sam and Mom a few hours ago. I check the rest of my texts, and by "the rest," I mean our friend group chat. There's nothing from Talia; she must still be on her date. My heart aches and I ignore it, swiping through the memes and videos I missed while I was asleep. Then, at the end of the group chat, Kev asks: What's the next step in the strategy? We gotta get you a date now Hayley, right?

I stare at the text. When Talia and I paused the strategy, we forgot to tell the others, and then I went and reactivated it at the concert when I freaked out. I know I could probably just tell them it's on hold, but if Talia is going to start dating Rose . . .

Well, it would probably help me get over my crush to find a date of my own.

Our final step was to hit up one of my teammates' birthday parties, I say. Half the team has summer birthdays, so someone usually hosts a blow-out. I'll do some recon.

Excellent, Kev says.

Jacob sends an emoji with sunglasses and a dancing man.

Bri replies with a GIF of some cartoon character twerking.

I send back a laughing emoji.

And Talia?

Nothing.

"Greetings, sister dearest," a voice says, and I yelp and drop my phone—luckily, only a few inches to the counter. Ella laughs as she passes me and grabs a snack bar from the cabinet.

"We need to put bells on you," I say.

She smirks and climbs into a chair beside me at the counter. "So. Sam."

"Right." I slowly spin my phone with both hands. "It's weird. She's not really much for avoiding things."

"Yeah, she's more of a mic-drop-and-walk-away type," Ella says around a mouthful of crunchy granola. "Do you think she's having problems with someone at camp?"

"I mean, camp's almost over. She seemed pretty peppy up until today. She was a little off on movie night, though."

"Yeah, I noticed. She got really quiet at the end of the night."

"She's been going to friends' houses a lot—"

"She *has* been doing that more and more the past few weeks." Ella nods. "I think it's one of her camp friends, too. So she'll probably stay with that friend until she can't avoid whatever's bothering her anymore."

"Huh." I rest my chin in my hand and stare out the window at the backyard. Dad's vegetable garden is going strong. "OK. But she can't miss Family Fun Friday."

"It's a sacred tradition," Ella says dryly.

"So we corner her then?" I ask.

"Yeah. After we go up to bed."

We fist bump and sit there together in silence for a minute.

"What about you?" Ella asks. Her voice is light—too light.

I side-eye her. "I'm fine."

"I'm just asking." She shrugs. "Also, I don't believe you. You've been moping around the house all week. Did the strategy flop or something?"

I grimace before I can hide my reaction.

"I knew it," she says.

"It didn't flop! Talia found someone. And I had that date with Mel. Even though it didn't go anywhere."

"Talia found someone? How's that going?"

"Great," I say. "They're on their second date right now. It's cute."

Ella laughs. "Hayley, you are such a bad liar."

"I'm not lying!" I glare at her. "You don't know everything."

"Sure," Ella says. "But I don't need to when you use that tone of voice. What's going on?"

"Nothing," I mumble.

She sighs. "Look. I know you're usually the avoider of the family, but don't make me run an intervention for you, too. Whatever it is is going to catch up with you eventually, so deal with it. Just some older sister advice."

My stomach twists at her words. I roll my eyes. "You're only two years older than me!"

She shrugs. "Just think about it."

CHAPTER SIXTEEN

THE NEXT MORNING, Talia still hasn't texted me.

Are you alive?? Is Rose a serial killer?? I text her, trying to ignore the sick feeling in my stomach.

Hi, I am alive! she replies within a minute. I had a really good time. I got home late for dinner and then I was so tired I just zoned out and fell asleep!

I roll over onto my back and stare at the ceiling for a moment, then pick up my phone. Do you wanna hang out later and tell me about it? I know it's going to hurt to hear about Rose, but at the same time, it would be weird if I didn't ask. And maybe this is a fake-it-till-you-make-it situation. The more I pretend like I'm fine and don't have a crush on my best friend, the more it will become true, and then everything can go back to feeling totally normal.

Yep. That's definitely how it works.

My phone pings. I would love to! Me and Kev were gonna meet up at World Pizza this afternoon, do you wanna join?

Sure!

Huh. Talia made plans without me. The day after her date. I don't know why this feels so weird. We all hang out together a lot, and of course my friends can hang out without me. I mean, Talia and I hang out just the two of us all the time.

But this is different. This is Talia's second date ever. And I'm her best friend. Shouldn't I be the first person she tells, no matter how tired she is? Shouldn't we already have plans, with Kev joining us, instead of the other way around?

I feel weird that I even feel weird about it, but I can't shake the feeling that something is off. Maybe this is what happens when you date. I've heard about people getting sucked into their relationships. I guess I never considered the possibility that it would happen with me and Talia.

Tears well up and I blink them back. I'm overreacting. I probably wouldn't even be this upset if I didn't have a crush on Talia. If I was a better friend, I'd be able to just be happy for her. If I was better at this whole romance thing, I'd be able to pick people who are actually attainable. I'd be able to turn off my feelings. I'd be able to shake off sixth grade and live in the present. I just turned sixteen. I'm almost a junior. It's stupid to still feel this way because of something that happened years ago.

I take deep breaths until my heart rate feels normal and the tears are gone, and then I get out of bed, grab my stuff and a protein bar, and head to practice.

"Hey, do you know if someone on the team is having a party this summer?" I ask Mariah as we warm up. Last summer was legendary; one of the graduating seniors was super rich and a Leo and invited everyone and their friends to her house for a pool party.

"Victoria's hosting it," she says, naming one of the varsity point guards. Victoria is super friendly, a little shorter than me, with curly red hair. "She's at one of the fancy camps this summer, but a friend of hers told everyone a few practices ago."

I frown. "I don't remember that."

"It was the day you were late," Mariah says, sinking a three-pointer.

"Oh." I press my fingers into the pebbly skin of the ball.

"It's in a few weeks, on August fifth, I think," Mariah says. "And we can bring anyone we want. She lives in that rich neighborhood down in Madison Valley, so it's gonna be lit."

"Sweet." I shake off the reminder of my mess-up last week and walk to center court. Mariah follows me, and so does Sherika, and slowly the other players join up for our morning huddle, still talking and laughing, dribbling or fidgeting with their basketballs.

I clap my hands. "OK, y'all!"

One of the varsity players glances at me, but the chatter doesn't die down.

"Let's go, Salmon!" Sherika yells, and it works like a charm. Most of the girls clap out the rhythm that follows the chant, and the group quiets down. She glances at me.

"Let's do some footwork drills," I say, and we all move, straggling into position at one end of the court. It's not as orderly as usual, but at least they're listening.

On my bus ride home, I scroll through basketball highlight videos. As I watch, I analyze the plays, think about what I would have done differently, and fantasize about my future.

I have no idea what I want to do with my life after high school, but I'm going to be a junior soon, so I'll have to start thinking seriously about it. The truth is, if I could do anything, it would be basketball. I'd get recruited for a top-tier college, with a full-ride scholarship, then get drafted into the WNBA after I graduate. But that's a one-in-a-million shot. I'd have to be really good, better than I am now, and my school would have to be the type that attracts college scouts. We get a few, and we do all right usually, but we're not known for our basketball program.

Sherika's face pops into my head—and that comment she made at our first summer practice: *You should be a coach.*

I have to admit, it felt good when she said that, and not just because I had a crush on her. I've been really enjoying leading our practices, even if the vibes were a little off today. Actually, they've been a little off ever since I was late. I know it was a mistake, that it could have happened to anyone, but *still*. I'm the keyholder, and I don't want to let my team down.

When I get home, I feel so tired, and it doesn't just feel like post-practice tired. That's a good tired. This feels heavier. I pound back a smoothie in the kitchen, then head upstairs to pick my outfit for my hang with Talia and Kev before I shower and head out again. Talia may not like me back, or even know that I have a crush, but I can still look as cute as possible. I know it'll help me feel a little better.

I'm ready and waiting on the couch when my doorbell rings an hour later. I chose a sunset orange crop top and a high-waisted denim skirt with pearly buttons down the front, plus my sandals. A cute summer look, accessorized with a tie-dye fanny pack and a jolt of anxiety in my chest. Good times!

I swing open the door, and Talia's there smiling at me. She looks head-to-toe amazing in a teal sundress and her curls up in a bun with a few strands framing her face. We hug, and I breathe in the scent of her lotion—it's citrusy. Normally she uses lavender-scented products, but this is new. Another new thing.

"I'm ready for pizza and details!" I say, extra excited to cover up how much smelling her just threw me off.

"Well, perfect, because I'm ready to tell you!" Talia claps her hands. I lock the door and we head down the street.

She's walking bouncier than usual, and I can't help grinning. "I'm guessing it went well?"

She holds a finger up to her lips. "I'll tell you everything once we're there."

"OK, fine." I pretend to pout, and she laughs.

About ten minutes later, we link up with Kev and head down Jackson Street toward the International District.

"How's Parker?" I ask. "Did their chest heal OK?"

"They're good," he says. "They had some complications for a minute. One of their nipples got infected." He pitches his voice lower when he says the last sentence, but an older gentleman passing us still gives us a look.

"Oh my god." I put a hand up to my mouth. Talia grimaces.

"Yeah, it was *not great*." Kev hits the button for the crosswalk signal, and a minute later we're crossing the intersection and heading down the hill toward Rainier Avenue. "They were fine; they didn't get sick or anything. It was just gross."

"Did it heal?" Talia asks.

"I mean . . ." Kev glances at us, smirking. "Kind of."

"OK, Mr. Mysterious." Talia rolls her eyes.

"Are you sure you wanna know?" he asks.

"Um, *yeah!*" we chorus and look at each other, laughing. This is the Talia and Hayley I'm used to. I'm starting to feel more at ease, less distracted by the way my hand keeps brushing against hers as we walk three across down the sidewalk.

"Well . . ." He pauses for dramatic effect, striding in front of us, then whirls around. "It *fell off!*"

"What?!"

"They straight up have a little crater where their nip used to be," he says, falling back into step beside us. "Apparently it happens sometimes. It's not a big deal. They healed up just fine otherwise, and they said it doesn't bother them, so . . ."

"Wow," I say.

"I've been calling them Ol' No-Nip," he says, grinning, and we burst out laughing.

When we walk into World Pizza and the smell of cheese and bread hits my nostrils, I suddenly realize how hungry I am.

The pizzas in the display case look fresh, and we each order slices in turn. I get a pepperoni—made with Field Roast meatless sausage, since all of their pizzas are vegetarian—a cheese with peach slices on top, and a plain cheese.

We slip into an empty booth, Talia on one side, Kev and I on the other.

Kev and I exchange glances, and we fix Talia with a stare.

"OK," he says. "Tea. Now."

She giggles. "OK, so. We met at Cal Anderson. They brought the snacks, and I brought the drinks. We set up on that hill at the north end, by the field where people bring their dogs."

We nod. I can see it in my mind. Rose and Talia, smiling at each other while puppies frolic around them. I take a big bite of my pizza and focus on what she's saying.

"They brought a tarot deck, and they gave me a reading about my past, present, and future." She wiggles her fingers like she's doing magic.

"Oh, so they're into witchy shit?" Kev asks.

"Yeah, they read tarot, and they're studying astrology, too," Talia says.

Rose sounds really cool. Definitely cooler than me. I can't even name a single tarot card, let alone tell Talia her future.

"So what did the cards say?" Kev asks.

"I can't remember," Talia says, blushing. "I kind of . . . was distracted. By how cute they were."

"Yes!" Kev fist pumps, glancing at me. I force a grin, like I'm loving this as much as he is.

Talia keeps talking, telling us about the snacks they brought, what they talked about together, how they got to play with a few of the dogs, and how Rose walked her home. Then she pauses.

"We didn't kiss," she says. "I think I wanted to? I'm not sure. But I do like them, and we've been texting about making plans again. Actually, Hayley, I was going to ask you about that."

"Me?" I hate how relieved I feel that Talia and Rose didn't kiss.

"Yeah, they have a friend who's single and seems really cool, so we were thinking of doing a double date?"

"Sure!" I say before I can stop myself.

"Hey, what about me?" Kev pokes out his lower lip.

"Their friends aren't into guys," Talia says.

Kev sighs dramatically. "It's all good. I guess me and Jacob still have our bromance."

I laugh along with them, but my head is spinning. *Why did I just say yes? Couldn't my brain just take one single second to think about something before jumping in?*

"Congrats," Kev says, turning to me with a hand lifted. "The strategy's almost complete." I stare at his hand for a second. He wiggles his fingers. "Don't leave me hanging."

I high-five him and look at Talia. She's smiling. *Maybe this will be fine. Maybe it'll be fun. A double date. Just like how I imagined.*

Great.

CHAPTER SEVENTEEN

THE NEXT MORNING, I'm dragging. It's not even that I'm tired. I slept fine—minus the dream where Talia and Rose got married and I was Talia's maid of honor and still in love with her, and all our friends turned into puppies, and I was running around trying to catch all of them. And the dream where Talia confessed her love and I woke up in the middle of the night ecstatic for five seconds until I realized it wasn't real. And the dream—

OK, so maybe I didn't sleep that great.

"Hayley!" Ella pounds on the bathroom door, and I almost drop my phone.

"Just a minute," I yell back. I don't even have the excuse of getting sucked into socials while I was on the toilet, because I was just zoned out, staring at the floor.

I come down the stairs in time to see Sam as she heads out. She's been at a friend's every night this week. She's usually pretty social, but that's way more than normal. Just as Ella predicted.

I'm not that hungry, but I grab a couple granola bars and stuff them into my bag. The coffee pot is still on, so I turn it off. There's about half a pot left, and I pour it into a jar for Mom and Dad to have iced coffee tomorrow if they want.

I stop mid-pour. I feel so heavy and all I want to do is crawl back in bed and mope about Talia.

Some coffee would help. Not a lot. Just a little.

I grab a small thermos from the cabinet, pour the rest of the coffee in, cap the jar, and grab the creamer from the fridge. Dad won't notice if I borrow a little bit.

I put the top on the thermos and race out the door to practice. I haven't checked my phone in a minute, but I think I'm on time.

The morning is a little cloudy; it's cooled down from last week, but Dad mentioned it's only supposed to last a few days before we get another heat wave. Climate change is really speeding up. The last few summers have all had heat waves, and I know it's a matter of time before wildfire season starts and the city disappears in a smoky haze for days at a time. But we still have it good compared to the folks who have to evacuate and watch their homes and towns burn down.

My brain is really on a roll this morning, playing the highlight reel of anxieties. I gulp down some coffee as I speedwalk down the path. I'm almost to the corner, just in time to hear a familiar sound: the roar of an approaching bus.

There it is. My bus zooms past, right in front of me. I break into a sprint, rounding the corner, but it blazes past my stop.

I race after it for two blocks, but the driver never slows. The bus leaves me in its literal dust at an intersection, rattling through just as the light turns red. I grind to a halt, breathing hard, and watch the cars pass in front of me.

I'm going to be late.

I trudge up to the next stop and text the practice group chat. If I'm lucky, if the next bus comes on time and traffic isn't bad, I'll only be twenty minutes late. Mariah and Sherika are the only ones who respond to my message.

It happens! Sherika says. We can jog on the track until you get here.

Mariah sends a running emoji.

The bus arrives a few minutes early, and I check my phone over and over for the entire ride, as if I can speed up time with sheer willpower. Students get on as we pass through Montlake, over the bridge, and into the University District; they all crowd on and off at the stops along the street in front of the University of Washington. And then it's just me, riding to the end of the line.

"Thank you!" I wave to the bus driver and hit the ground running the rest of the way. By the time the back of the school comes into sight, I'm winded, but not too bad. I guess all these mornings of running lines are working.

I'm here! I text the group chat, then fumble with the keys, unlock the door, and speed across the gym to the gear closet. I don't know why I'm still running, but it feels like I need to. I get the closet open and drag out the ball bin, just as the girls file in, sweaty from their warm-up down at the track.

It's not just a few varsity girls who side-eye me this time. Some JV girls do, too. I'm even getting a few open glares. My shoulders tense. *I wasn't even that late. And they did their warm-up, so what's the big deal?*

"You OK?" Sherika comes up and starts grabbing balls out, tossing them to the girls, her face concerned. "You look stressed."

"I feel like everyone's mad at me," I say, pitching my voice low so the others won't hear. I sound like a whiny little kid, but I can't stop myself. This is why I don't drink coffee; when I do, my filter disappears. It's not good.

"They'll get over it," Sherika says. "You want me to lead today? So you have a minute to settle in?"

"Sure." I shrug and head over to the sidelines to drop my stuff.

The coffee's gone, and I'm not tired anymore, even after all the running. My heart is still racing. I take a long drink of water as the other girls shoot baskets and Sherika cranks up a bright and poppy playlist. I watch as the girls loosen up, joking around with each other. They don't look that annoyed anymore. *Sherika's a genius; what a sneaky way to shift the energy.*

I take deep breaths, trying to slow my heartbeat. I want to let the music change my mood, too, but instead it just makes my chest tighter. It's so loud.

I grab a ball and join Mariah at a hoop with a few other girls.

"What happened this morning?" Mariah dribbles over to me. "You out partying again?" She grins.

I force a smile. I know she's just teasing. "Nah, I barely missed the bus."

"That's shitty. I'm sorry." She squares up and fires off a perfect fadeaway jump shot. *Swish.*

I follow suit. *Clank.* My ball bounces off the rim and comes back to me.

"Are you mad?" I ask.

She shakes her head. "Nah. It's whatever. I mean, it's a little annoying. This is the second time."

"I'm sorry."

"We just all depend on you for this practice time," she says, turning to me. "I don't know what's going on, but you've never been late to a practice. Like, ever. I know we aren't besties, but you're my teammate, and I know how much you love this sport. I just wonder if it's still important to you or if there's something else going on."

"It's definitely still important to me," I say, fidgeting with the ball, tossing it back and forth. "It's honestly just a mistake."

She looks at me for a long moment, and I stare back. It's not a tense moment, but she definitely looks skeptical. I don't know what to tell her, though. There's nothing to tell. I overslept after the concert, and today, I just left a little too late.

"OK," she says, shrugging.

The music's turned down, and Sherika calls us in from the center court. I jog over to stand beside her and nod along as she takes the lead. All the girls are looking at her. Nobody's watching me. I should feel happy they're not still glaring at me, but this is almost worse. Now it feels like they're ignoring me. Like all the trust and leadership I built up this summer is just gone.

I swallow the lump in my throat. I can't cry now. I have to keep my head in the game.

By Friday night, the tension at basketball practice isn't the only reason I'm on edge. Talia's working on planning our double date, and she texts me all day—something I would normally love—to get my answers for date, time, and place. It turns out we're all free tomorrow morning, which feels way too soon, but I can't tell Talia that. She seems so excited, and I don't want to let her down.

At family dinner, my phone buzzes again. I sneak a look while Ella chatters about something that happened at work.

OMG, Rose suggested Cafe Flora! Talia says. My chest tightens. That's our favorite brunch spot, the place we go whenever we have allowance money saved up. I don't want to share it with Rose and their friend. But there's no way to say that without sounding completely unhinged.

And I'm being silly anyway. It's just a restaurant, and Talia's my best friend. I need to get over this crush and be happy for her, and this will help.

It has to.

Sweet! I text back. Who's my date?

"Hayley." I look up and Mom arches an eyebrow at me. "Phone."

"Sorry." I slide it back in my pocket and try to focus on my food. Dad made pasta, and everyone else is half-done except for me and Sam. She's been quiet all night, her face sunburned from whatever she did after camp with her friends yesterday. One by one, she winds the noodles around her fork and eats them, her eyes glazed out like she's on another planet entirely. Her buzzcut has grown out a little; it's now a soft cap of short brown hair above her round face.

"What is it?" Dad asks her. "Food OK?"

She nods.

"Tastes great, honey," Mom says. "This time."

"I agree," he says reflectively. "It's less soggy worm and more . . . firm worm."

"Dad." Ella puts her fork down. "Gross."

While they banter, I eat another forkful of pasta. Dad tossed it with spinach, sun-dried tomatoes, feta, and his signature sauce, a concoction of nutritional yeast, soy sauce, apple cider vinegar, garlic, and water. He says it's supposed to be a salad dressing, but it works on everything—you name it, he's tried it.

My phone vibrates against my thigh and my heart jolts. It's probably Talia texting me about my date. Mom and Dad are busy listening to Ella talk more, so I take another peek.

Oh right, I should probably tell you that lol, Talia says. Her name's Brenna. She volunteers at the animal shelter on weekends and apparently she's obsessed with pop culture stuff. Movies, music, celebrities etc. So you'll have plenty to talk about. She adds an emoji with its tongue sticking out.

LOL nice, I text back. It's the exact opposite of how I feel.

When we're all done, Mom cleans up and the rest of us head to the living room and gather around the game cabinet, but Sam hangs back, watching us. Dad tries to include her, asking her opinion on the games we pull out, but she just shrugs. When we finally settle on one of our favorites—a horror-themed game where the characters are trapped in a haunted mansion and one of them goes rogue—Sam just stands there, shifting from foot to foot while we set up.

I argue with Ella over who gets to play which token, and when I look up, Sam's gone.

Dad sees my questioning look. "Sam's going to sit this one out," he says, forehead crinkled slightly. "She's feeling tired and wants to rest."

Ella and I nod. When Dad goes to check on Mom, we both look at each other. I was so wrapped up in my anxiety about the double date that I completely forgot about what Ella and I had planned for tonight. We were going to corner Sam after game night and find out what's been bothering her. Now I feel extra bad. Sam was obviously checked out all evening, and all I could think about was myself.

"We're still on, right?" I ask. "She's clearly not tired."

"Oh yeah." Ella nods. "That's a red herring if I've ever heard one."

"Red herring?" I snort. "You sound like an old-timey detective."

"It's not my fault I have a better vocabulary than you," she shoots back.

"Just because you're obsessed with Agatha Christie books—" I start, but then our parents walk in. Ella gives me a meaningful look. I give her one back. After the game, it's go time.

"Aaaaaand you're dead!" Ella shouts as she kills off Mom's character. "I win!"

Mom clutches her chest. "Betrayed by the traitor among us!"

Dad and I laugh. Ella killed us off a while ago, and we've been watching Mom dodge across the board one step ahead of her, trying unsuccessfully to defeat her and escape the mansion.

"OK, you goblins," Dad says, leaning back. "It's getting late."

That's our cue: we pack up the board and head upstairs to let Mom and Dad have their weekly check-in time. They've been doing it as long as I can remember: thirty minutes every week where they talk about what went well in their relationship, any sticking points or possible issues, and whatever else helps them be good partners to each other. It doesn't mean they never fight—I hear them bicker from time to time, and sometimes they have to go in their room, shut the door, and spend time working something out—but Mom says the check-in helps them avoid little issues turning into big ones.

It's something I want in my future relationship. If I ever have one. My heart twinges, and I check my phone. Nothing else from Talia. I have to admit Brenna sounds cool.

But she's not Talia.

"You ready?" Ella whispers.

I come back down to earth. The upstairs hallway is dark, and the light is shining from underneath Sam's door. I nod. Ella taps on the door.

"Hey, Sam, I have a question for you."

A moment goes by, and Sam answers in her cranky voice. "Can it wait?"

"No."

"Fine."

Ella opens the door and we both slip in, shutting it behind us. Sam's eyes widen and she sits up straight, laptop falling off her stomach onto the bed. High-pitched cartoon character voices chatter from the speakers and she hits the space bar, silencing it.

"You tricked me!"

"It's not hard." Ella shrugs. I elbow her. We're here to help Sam, not antagonize her.

"We're worried about you," I say.

"I'm fine." She glares at us. "Get out of my room."

Normally we would, but these are extenuating circumstances. I glance at Ella, and she nods.

"You've been off all week. I saw you crying that one morning, and you've avoided us ever since, going to friends' houses every day." She opens her mouth, but I barrel on. "I respect that you want us to get out of your room, and we'll leave if you really want us to, but you don't have to push us away. We're your sisters and we love you—even if we annoy the shit out of you sometimes."

That gets a little smirk from her.

"We just want you to know we have your back," Ella says.

I nod. "And if you're feeling depressed, or something's going on with your friends, you can tell us."

"Even if you're into drugs," Ella says.

"Not *even if*," I hiss. "That's so pathologizing. There's nothing wrong with trying drugs," I say to Sam. "*And* if it's not going well, we're here for you."

"We'll probably also have to tell Mom and Dad," Ella adds. "But yeah. We're here for you."

"I'm not doing drugs," Sam says, rolling her eyes.

"Is Corey being mean to you again?" I ask. A few years ago, Sam's best friend, Corey, was going through some family stuff and took it out on Sam. They argued all the time, and Corey even spread a rumor about Sam at school. The guidance counselor had to get involved, there were parent meetings—it was a whole thing.

"No, we're fine." Sam fiddles with the comforter, looking away from us. "Corey's been really great, actually."

"Do you . . ." I examine her face. Her cheeks are red, eyes a bit glassy. She was definitely crying earlier. "Do you have a crush on—"

"No! Oh my god, no. It's not that. They've just been . . . supporting me." Sam's running the comforter between her fingers over and over.

I move closer and sit on the end of the bed, and Ella sits down on the carpet. "Supporting you with what?"

"I . . ." Sam twists her mouth around, very firmly not looking at us. "I . . . um . . ."

I know what she's about to say before she says it, like a door unlocking somewhere in my brain. As she runs a hand over her head, I remember all the middle-school days I spent running to the bathroom to hide my anxiety. How alone and anxious I felt, how I didn't know whether I could trust anyone I knew with the truth.

"I've been using they/them pronouns at camp," Sam says. "And it ended this week, and it really sucks because everyone there was so cool about it, and I know you all would be about it, too, but there's always a *chance* that you won't be—like this one kid thought their dad would be fine with them being nonbinary because their older sister was gay, but then their dad was all weird about it—" Sam's face is getting redder, tears welling in her—their—eyes.

"Sam." Ella's voice is quiet, but Sam stops, finally lifting their eyes to look at her. Ella smiles. "I'm so proud of you. I know Mom and Dad will be, too. I mean, Dad shaved your head, remember?"

Sam nods.

"You're my sibling for life," I say. "I'm so proud of you. Do you want a hug?"

They nod and crawl over to me. I wrap my arms around them and they squeeze back, starting to sniffle. "Thank you," they say, voice muffled against my shoulder.

"No need to thank us," I say. I don't want Sam to ever feel alone and scared the way I did in middle school. Now that they're letting us in, I want them to know we have their back.

Ella sits down on Sam's other side. "Big sister sandwich." She squeezes Sam and they giggle.

When Sam starts to shift, we both pull back. They wipe their face with the hem of their shirt. "When do you think I should tell Mom and Dad?"

"Whenever you want," I say. "We can switch it up subtly in front of them till you do, if you want. Or just avoid pronouns altogether."

Sam chews on the inside of their cheek for a second, then nods. "If you could just avoid pronouns and gendered words, that would be great."

"You got it."

We sit there for a second and I squeeze their hand. They squeeze back. Ella squeezes their other hand, and then we're all squeezing back and forth and giggling like a chain reaction.

They glance over at their laptop. "Do you wanna stay and watch cartoons?"

Ella nods. "Absolutely."

"Yes, please," I add.

A few minutes later, we're all set up in a nest of pillows. Sam presses play, and with a big sigh, they lean back and settle in.

CHAPTER EIGHTEEN

TALIA'S MOM DRIVES us to brunch the next morning. I try to act normal, but I'm hyper-aware of Talia the second I slide into the backseat. She twists to smile back at me, and it's like she's glowing from within. I can smell her conditioner—back to lavender—and her skin is tanned from all the time we've been spending in the sun.

"I can't wait to double date with you," she says.

"Same!" I chirp. I sound so fake, but she turns back around like she doesn't notice anything.

As we head toward Café Flora, my stomach jolts with every bump we hit. I try to do my breathing exercises, and they help a little bit, but when we pull up to the café, anxiety spikes in my chest again. I scan the brunch crowd waiting outside for tables, but I don't see Rose.

"OK, girls." Talia's mom turns and looks at us. "I want you to have this." She holds out a credit card.

"Oh no, it's OK," I say, but she shakes her head.

"It's my pleasure. I'm just so excited for you both. Dating is such a milestone."

"*Mom.*" Talia covers her face.

"Don't 'Mom' me. You're growing up! And you both look so beautiful."

"It's just a date, not a wedding," Talia says.

"Still." Her mom waves a hand. "It's on me."

Talia takes the card, and we slide out. When the car pulls away, Talia wiggles the card at me.

"Thrifting rampage later?" she asks. Her eyes are gleaming.

"Oh definitely," I say. "Round trip to Paris after?"

"Oui oui, mademoiselle!"

We're giggling, throwing out more and more ridiculous scenarios, when Talia's gaze shifts past me and she breaks out into a big grin. I turn, and there they are.

Rose and Brenna.

Rose is shorter than I remember; I didn't really get a good read on their height at the salon. Their hair is still the same pixie cut, like mine is now. But this time theirs is dyed a perfect shade of pastel pink. Like mine was a few months ago.

Their outfit even kind of looks like mine: I'm wearing a pink tank top with a floral print shirt tied at my waist and light denim shorts, and they're wearing a black tank under a floral print shirt with black denim shorts. They're wearing fishnets and big boots, and I'm wearing my sandals.

Rose is kind of like me but make it vaguely goth. I wonder if they play any sports.

Their friend—Brenna—smiles at me. She's short and curvy with long light brown hair. "Hi! You must be Hayley."

I stretch out a hand. "And you're Brenna."

"That's me." She toys with her earrings. They're little donuts with pink frosting and sprinkles.

"Those are amazing."

"Thanks. I made them."

"No way." I move closer and she spins them around, showing them off.

"They were my final project in ceramics last year."

"That's so cool." I glance over at Talia and Rose and my heart leaps into my throat. They're holding hands, and Rose is gazing at Talia, who's blushing.

"Hey!" My voice comes out louder than I intended, and they both look up, startled. I smile to soften it. "Should we get some brunch?"

With a chorus of "yes" and "I'm starving," we move into the entryway of the restaurant. The host takes Talia's name and says we'll have to wait for a while, so we file back outside and find a spot to stand by the café windows.

Even though there's a small crowd outside, we must have come at the end of a wave, because one by one the other groups get called in for a table, and sooner than I thought, the host is leading us inside.

To our left is a more traditional restaurant layout. Two rows of tables run parallel to each other next to the big bright windows filled with plants, along with a row of tables along the back wall and a counter with high stools. Art by local artists hangs above the tables. In front of us is a corridor with more tables leading to the outdoor patio. We follow the host to the right, into my favorite part of the restaurant.

It's a room encircled in windows, with the triangle jut of a greenhouse roof above and a water fountain in the center shadowed by a small tree and more plants. The floor is gray stone tile, like we're in a garden courtyard, except we're inside. All the windows are open, letting in the warm summer breeze. Tables line the perimeter, with a few placed on either side of the water feature.

All the tables are filled except one, just inside the entrance to the room. The host seats us, hands out menus, and then hurries back to the front of the restaurant.

I breathe in deep. The smell of earth and water mixes with the sweet and savory scent of breakfast food: syrup, pancakes, eggs, biscuits, roasted vegetables, and more. My mouth waters and my stomach growls so loud Talia snorts and glances over at me. I smirk at her. Rose and Brenna don't seem to notice.

"Wow." Rose scans the room. "This place is gorgeous. I see why it's your favorite." They smile at Talia.

"We've been coming here for ages," I say. "It's, like, our spot." I smile at Talia, too, and she smiles back.

"Talia told me you two are besties," Rose says.

Warmth blooms in my chest. Talia talked about me to Rose. I wonder what else she said.

"I mean, yeah," I say. "We go way back." *I sound so cool and collected. This is good. I just need to keep this up for the whole date.*

"That's one way to put it," Talia says, arching an eyebrow at me.

"You were born on the same day, in the same hospital, right?" Rose looks from Talia to me.

"Whoa!" Brenna says. "I can't think of any friends I've had that long."

I nod at Rose. "Our parents still have dinners together once a month."

"That's so cute," they say.

The server, a tall blond person with tattoos all over their arms and neck, approaches the table. "How we doing today?"

We answer in a vague affirmative chorus and shuffle with our menus.

"Do you wanna share?" Talia asks Rose. "A sweet thing and a savory thing?"

That's what she and I always do when we're here. *Not today though, I guess.*

"Sure!" Rose says, scanning the menu. "What about this?"

Talia looks over. "Ooh, sounds great. And . . ."

I wait for her to say it, taking a deep breath. *It's fine. Talia can order whatever she wants with whoever she wants.*

"Waffles?"

What? We always get pancakes. First the new ice cream flavor, then the new shampoo, and now this. They're small things, but they're also not. I've known Talia, her routines, her favorites, for years. They've never changed, but now . . .

I'm sitting, but I feel unsteady. I stare at the menu, trying to focus on the options, trying to figure out what to get now that I have to order on my own.

Brenna nudges me. "You wanna share something, too?"

"Oh!" I look at her, and then back at my menu. "Yeah. OK. What were you thinking?"

We end up getting pancakes, because I need something to stay the same today, and a scramble. While we wait for food, the three of them chatter away, and I try to keep up and stay interested. I should give Brenna a chance. She's cute, and she seems really sweet.

Talia and Rose drift off into conversation about astrology, Rose explaining something about how all the houses work. I like astrology, but I'm not in that deep, and I can't follow what they're talking about. At the same time, our food comes and a wave of relief washes over me. The sooner we eat, the sooner this date will be over.

"So how do you and Rose know each other?" I ask Brenna as we dig in.

"Well . . ." Brenna glances at Rose, but they're totally engrossed in talking to Talia, giggling about whatever she just said. "We dated. Just for a minute," she says quickly, and my eyebrows rise before I can stop myself. "It totally didn't work. We weren't attracted to each other. It was more of a friend vibe, so . . . here we are."

I glance at Talia again. *Has everyone dated their friend and then broken up?* She's nodding along with whatever Rose is saying. The sun filtering through the trees casts a dappled light across both of them. They look great together. They look like a couple.

"Hayley?"

I look back to Brenna. Her head's tilted a bit.

"Sorry, I spaced. What were you saying?" I stab a few pieces of pancake and take a bite.

"Oh, I just asked you what you do for fun. Rose told me you play basketball?"

I nod, chewing and swallowing the food. "Mhmm. I've played since middle school." Normally I'd be all over this subject, but today, it just reminds me of being late on Thursday and the crawling embarrassment of watching the girls file in, side-eyeing me and whispering to each other.

"What position?"

"Power forward or shooting guard," I say, and then I have to explain what each one does and how basketball works because it turns out Brenna isn't sporty at all. I keep waiting for the light bulb to click on, to feel that glow I normally do when I talk about basketball, but it just doesn't happen.

Then Brenna starts telling me about her family and I try to listen. It's hard, though. Rose is a loud talker, and I'm struggling to shut out their voice along with all the other sounds of the restaurant: forks clinking, people chattering, the quiet music that I can somehow hear every word of. It doesn't help that whenever I look over at the two of them, I get distracted by the way Rose is looking at Talia, or teasing her about something, or pointing out something in the room or outside.

Maybe it would be awkward if Talia and I tried to date. Maybe we wouldn't have any chemistry, like Rose and Brenna didn't.

But when I think about kissing her, my insides feel like carbonated water, fizzing and popping. That's a good sign, right?

It doesn't matter, though, if she doesn't want it—and I can tell she doesn't. She's too interested in whatever Rose is talking about now.

My eyes fill up with tears. Oh no. What's happening?

"Hayley?" I turn slowly. Brenna's staring at me, her eyebrows drawn together. "Are you OK?"

I open my mouth, but no sound comes out. I look at Talia and Rose. They're silent all of a sudden, both of them turned toward me. I mumble something that I hope sounds like "I'll be right back," push back my chair, squeeze past Brenna, and beeline for the bathroom at the other side of the restaurant.

Inside the bathroom, I lock myself in a stall and focus on my breathing—counting four in, four out; four in, six out; four in, eight out; deep into my belly—but it doesn't work. The breath gets caught in my chest where it feels like a giant hand is squeezing my ribcage. All the sound around me is dimming.

I have to get out of here.

I head out of the bathroom, through the restaurant toward the door. Everything is going fast and slow at the same time, like trying to run in a dream. I hear my name, and then Talia's there, blocking the doorway.

"I have to go," I say, stopping short in front of her.

"What? Why? What's wrong?" Her hands are clutched together in front of her, like she's pleading.

I open my mouth, but nothing comes out.

"Is everything OK?" Rose pops up behind Talia, Brenna close behind. I look from one to the other, and back to Talia, but I can't think of anything say.

So I brush past Talia and run out.

I hear Talia call my name again, but I'm in a full sprint up the sidewalk, people dodging out of my way as I go. Part of me is screaming NO STOP GO BACK, but it's too late. I can't take it back. I have to go. I ruined everything, and this is the only thing I can do.

I run until my sides are aching and I'm wheezing, and then I run a little longer, until I finally slow to a trudge. I'm far away from the restaurant now—or at least, far enough.

Houses line the street on either side of me, tall wide-branched trees keeping the sidewalk shady and cool. A toddler babbles somewhere; a dog barks. I cut over toward the busier street nearby and cross to the closest bus stop, the bus Talia and I would have taken if her mom hadn't driven us. A few minutes later, one pulls up, and I get on, keeping my eyes down as I head to a seat in the back. I'm crying and sweaty, and the last thing I need is sympathy from a stranger.

I pull out my phone, just out of habit, and now that I'm not running, I can see my notifications are blowing up. Talia's already called me multiple times, and as I hold the phone, she calls me again and again, texting me in between.

Where are you??

Are you OK??

Answer me

I can see the ellipses Hayley. I know you're there. Please tell me what's going on

I read every text as they come in. My heart isn't sinking; it's already at the bottom of the ocean, burrowing into the sediment inside the deepest trench, where nothing but darkness lives. My head is fuzzy, thoughts ping-ponging without rest.

Then Kevin texts me. Dude are you OK? Talia just told us—

Another text interrupts me as I read Kevin's. This time it's Bri. Hey are you— I close the thread midsentence.

Then Jacob. I don't even open it.

Talia probably texted them to tell them what happened. A new group chat, without me. Maybe Rose can join it. The thought fills my eyes with tears.

My friends keep texting me, and Talia keeps calling. Every time my phone vibrates, I jump, but I can't put it away, and I can't stop staring at the screen. I feel sick. *I'm a terrible friend. They're all worried about me and I'm ignoring them. I don't deserve them. Even if I answered now, what would I say? I can't tell any of them I have a crush on Talia.*

So this is happening, then. I'm going to ruin all of my friendships, not just with Talia but with everyone. Maybe it's better this

way. I'm clearly not capable of handling my shit. She deserves a better best friend. I should just walk away and let her fall in love in peace.

Then my mom calls me. I dismiss the first call, and she texts me immediately. Hayley, you did not just send me to voicemail. Answer my next call, or you're grounded. Basketball included.

Two seconds later, she calls again. I pick up.

"Hayley, I just got this frantic call from Talia that you ran out of the restaurant? You were crying? Where are you? I'm getting in the car now."

"No, don't! I'm on the bus home," I say in a low voice. I don't want the other people on the bus to hear how upset I am.

"What happened?"

"I can't . . ." My throat closes up. "I don't know."

"Hayley." There's a long pause, and she lets out a sigh. "OK. Which stop are you getting off at?"

I tell her.

"Stay on the phone with me and I'll meet you there," she says. "If I'm not there when you get there, *wait.* Don't go anywhere. I can still ground you."

"OK." I'm halfway between receding panic and the onset of post-anxiety exhaustion. I can't even protest. You need words to do that, and talking right now takes everything I have.

I put my phone on speaker in case she says something else and check my texts again. I should text my friends back, but every time I open one of the threads, I freeze up. None of them can know I have a crush on Talia.

Your mom let me know you were OK. Hayley, please talk to me, Talia says.

And:

What's wrong? Is it something I did? If you didn't want to go on the double date, you could have told me, I'd never make you do something you don't want to do.

And:

Please. Tell me what's going on.

Tears sting my eyes as she texts me over and over, but I'm too frozen to write back. I look out the window and recognize the houses around us just in time to pull the cord for my stop. The driver brakes hard, throwing me forward. I stumble out of the back doors and look around as the bus pulls away.

"Hayley!" My mom's voice echoes across the street. She runs to me, pulling me into a tight hug, then takes my hand and leads me up the block toward our house. I haven't held her hand since I was a kid, but I let it happen. It's kind of comforting.

"Sweetie, you look like a deer in the headlights," she says as we turn the corner onto our street. "Did you have a panic attack?"

I nod. I'm pretty sure that's what happened.

"That hasn't happened in a long time, right?" she says.

I shake my head.

From my peripheral vision, I see her look at me, but I don't meet her gaze. "I respect that you don't want to talk about it, and I'll let you have some time to calm down, but we can't have you running out of places like that," she says. "I'll give you some time to rest, but I want to talk to you tomorrow after family brunch, OK?"

I nod my head. Family brunch sounds like the last thing I want to do right now, but maybe I'll feel better in the morning.

Maybe.

Probably not.

CHAPTER NINETEEN

'M THE LAST one down to brunch the next morning. When I come in, there's a slight pause in the bustle. It's not like they all turn to stare at me, but I can tell they all feel me come in, and they're trying to act normal.

Mom smiles at me. "Hi, sweetie. Here's a plate."

I take it from her and sit down at the table. Sam helps Dad bring the food out. I can feel them looking at me, but I don't meet their eyes, tracing my finger over the blue flowers painted on the white ceramic. Mom made them in her pottery class last year.

Ella sits across from me and nudges my foot gently with hers. I move mine away. I know they're all worried, but in this moment, it just feels overwhelming. I'm already embarrassed about my panic attack yesterday; I can't hold my family's worry, too.

I move my hand to the pocket of my shorts without thinking and realize I left my phone upstairs. Eventually my friends stopped texting and calling last night, but they started again this morning. I want to text someone back, but when I picked up the phone, I didn't know how to start. So I set it back on my nightstand. I feel weirdly lost without it, but it's better than feeling like I have a bomb in my pocket.

I lift my eyes and take in the spread Dad cooked this morning. A mountain of huge, fluffy waffles sits on a platter in the center, with toppings grouped around it: chopped strawberries, peanut butter, frozen blueberries, whipped cream, and syrup. There's a plate of sausage patties and one of vegan bacon strips and a big bowl of scrambled eggs. Orange juice and almond milk sit at either end.

Normally Dad says something silly to kick us off, but today, he just smiles, his eyes lingering on me. I look away.

"I know it's just another Sunday, but it really is special to have brunch with all of you girls every week," he says.

"I'm glad all of us kids are here, too," Ella says, emphasizing the gender-neutral term ever so slightly, and we make eye contact across the table. I glance at Sam. Their leg is bouncing up and down, but they're smiling down at the table.

We pass the food around and I fill my plate. The day after a panic attack is always a hungry day.

"Actually, I have something to tell you," Sam says as soon as the last plate gets set back in the center of the table. I look at them, and everyone else does too. Their cheeks are slightly pink, and their hands are shaking a little as they hold their fork. They set it down and clasp their hands under the table, fixing their eyes on Mom and Dad. "Hayley and Ella already know this, but I'm nonbinary, and I want you to use they/them pronouns for me."

I look at my parents. Dad's face breaks into a wide grin, and Mom's eyes get misty. They both gaze at Sam with so much pride, the same pride I can see in Ella's face and feel in my chest, even though I'm worn out and still anxious.

"You got it, kiddo," Dad says.

"Do you want us to change the other words we use for you, too?" Mom asks.

Sam nods.

"OK, let's see," Mom says. "Sibling instead of sister. Kid instead of daughter. Kids for all of you together." She smiles at us.

"How do you want to handle the extended family?" Dad asks.

Sam scrunches up their nose. "Could you tell them?"

"Of course." He reaches out a hand, and Sam puts theirs in his. "I'm so glad you told us."

"Thanks," Sam said. They take a deep breath and let it out. "Can we talk about something else now?"

They all laugh, and I smile a little bit, too. It's a classic Sam response. Ella pipes up with some drama at her job—a customer who was rude to her the other day, and the manager had to intervene. I focus on my food, and the conversation moves on.

After brunch, I head upstairs to my room. When I glance at my phone screen, the number of messages is overwhelming. I turn it facedown.

I've only been lying on my bed scrolling through TV shows for a few minutes when Mom pokes her head around my half-open door.

"Hey." I shut my laptop and sit up as she closes the door. I forgot we were going to talk.

"Hi, you." She picks her way through the path to my bed and sits by my feet. She grabs one of them, shaking my leg, and I try to smile, but it feels forced. "So. You don't have to tell me what happened, but we do need to make a plan in case this happens again."

"I'm sorry," I say, small and whispery. "I just freaked out."

"You don't have anything to apologize for," Mom says. "I just want to know how to help you."

"I don't know," I say. My nose stings and tears well up. I press my palms to my eyes.

"Do you want to talk to me about what's been going on?"

I fiddle with the bedspread. The words are bottled in my throat, a pressure valve waiting for release. I've been keeping this in, and I can't anymore. I don't have to tell my friends, but I can tell Mom. I take a deep breath, and then it's all spilling out.

"I have a crush on Talia, and I don't know how or when it happened, maybe I was just oblivious, but it hit me at the concert, and then I pushed her to talk to Rose even though she didn't really want to, and now they're dating, and I wish it was me, but they look perfect together, and maybe it would just be better for Talia if I wasn't in the picture at all, but I wish we'd never made up this stupid summer love strategy, but I'm also happy for her, because I *want* her to be happy, but also I want her to be happy with *me*!" The last word wails out of my chest from somewhere deep, and I press a hand to my sternum, right where my heart aches, because I have to give up my best friend and it's all my fault.

"Oh, sweetie." My mom scoots closer. She wraps her arms around me as I sling my legs over her lap and lean against her chest, sobbing. I feel like a kid again, like I'm eleven and everyone is talking about the famous guys they think are cute and giggling about boys at school and all I can think about is—

"It's just like Leia," I mumble. The girl I had a crush on in sixth grade, the girl I couldn't tell anyone about, the girl who barely even knew I was alive.

"I haven't heard that name in a long time," Mom says, rubbing my back as she holds me. "Why does it feel like Leia?"

"Because." I take a few shallow, shaky breaths. "I like Talia, and I can't tell anyone. But this time, it's even worse, because if I do tell her, and something goes wrong, I'll lose my best friend—and probably all of my other friends, too."

"Like you were afraid of losing us back then?" Mom asks quietly.

I start sobbing again and she squeezes me tighter, murmuring to me as I do. Her words come through as if from far away, but they come through all the same: *I love you. I hear you. I'm sorry it's so hard. I'm so proud of you. I'm here.*

After a while, the sobs shrink into shuddering breaths, and I'm able to sit back up. Mom moves my legs off hers gently and grabs the box of tissues on my desk. I take one and blot my eyes.

"Keeping such a big secret is a lot of pressure," Mom says. "You've always had Talia to tell before."

I nod and blow my nose.

"I'll be right back," Mom says. A moment later I hear water running, and she comes back in with a damp washcloth. She puts one hand up to my cheek, patting my face with the other. I close my eyes. It's nice to be taken care of.

"Do you think you might be able to tell one of your friends? Maybe Bri?" she asks after a moment.

"I don't know." I take the washcloth from her and lay back, covering my face. "Once I tell one person, it'll be harder to keep it secret."

"Sometimes sharing a secret can lighten the weight of it, though," Mom says. "When we hide things, we have to carry the shame and anxiety, too. That can make things feel worse than they might be."

"I guess."

"And I know now," Mom says. "So you're not alone anymore."

I pull the washcloth off my face and look at her. Her eyes are warm, and it settles me. "Thanks."

"Of course."

We rest in silence for a while, her hand on my foot. The bed is soft underneath me, and there's a light breeze coming in through the window.

"Maybe in the future I could text or call you if I'm starting to panic?" I say. "And tell you where I am?"

"That's a good start," Mom says. "If your anxiety is really bothering you again, we can also talk to the doctor about medication and find you another therapist. There's no shame in that."

"That's true." I stare at the silhouettes of tree branches on my ceiling, cast there by the sunlight, waving gently back and forth. I don't know what it's like not to live with some level of anxiety. *Would I be able to just do things without overthinking them? Sounds fake, but OK.*

"Think about it," Mom says. "I want you to start carrying a little anxiety first-aid bag, too. Some fidget toys, something scented you like, reminders that will help ground you."

"OK." I prop myself on one elbow. "I was thinking, too. I know the therapist back in middle school told me to find private space to do my breathing. But when I was in the bathroom, I just started to feel trapped. Maybe I should try going outside next time instead?"

"As long as you contact me, too," Mom says.

"I will."

"Good." She smiles at me. "Dad and I were going to tackle some yard work projects this afternoon. Getting outside and getting your mind off things could be good for you." She glances at my phone. Alerts have been sounding on and off the whole time.

I know I should text people back. I could ask Mom to help me figure out what to say and sit here while I do it.

The wall is going up, though, between me and the task. It's that opposing magnet feeling again; I know I have to do it, and so I just can't.

I look at Mom and nod. "OK."

She smacks my shin lightly. "That's my girl. See you outside in five."

Monday morning, I make it to my bus with plenty of time, which is good, because if I'm late again I'll definitely have another panic attack. I still haven't texted Talia or any of our friends back yet. I've stopped opening the threads entirely, and the unread messages feel like lead weights in my mind. The more I try not to think about them, the heavier they get.

I close my eyes, turn up the music in my headphones, and run basketball plays in my head for the rest of the ride. At least I can still count on that.

At my stop, I head through the quiet neighborhood toward our school. Even though I don't love waking up early, there's something sweet about the morning. The air smells fresh, the light filters through the trees, the coffee shops and boutiques are just opening their doors; it makes me feel calmer, like everything might turn out OK. Eventually. Maybe.

No one's at the gym as I walk up. I'm on time, so there's still fifteen minutes to spare before my teammates arrive. I sling my backpack around to my front and rummage through the side pocket for my keys.

Nothing.

I check the other front pockets, and then once more, heart kicking into high gear. *This can't be happening.* I set my bag down and rifle through it, feeling all the way around the bottom. There's no jingle, no feel of cool metal in my fingers, just the grit of crumbs and lint.

I pull everything out of every compartment: my water bottle, my snack bars, my wallet, the change of clothes and towel that's been in my backpack since the start of the summer in case I ever decide I want to shower after practice, the crumpled papers from past essays and tests that I never cleaned out at the end of the year. I dump the backpack upside down, but all that falls out are those crumbs. I pat the pockets of my basketball shorts, but I already know what's happened.

I left my keys at home.

Crouched on the ground in front of all my things and my empty backpack, I curse, pressing my hands against my face.

"Hayley?"

I look up.

"You OK?" Sherika's eyes are soft and concerned. *Of course she'd be the one to find me hunched on the ground like a goblin.*

"I . . ." I stop for a minute and take a deep breath. I'm already choking up. I really don't want to cry in front of my teammates, especially the varsity players. "I forgot the keys."

"Ohhhhh." Sherika's eyebrows go up. "So that means—"

"No practice." I stand up slowly, staring down at my backpack.

Behind me I hear a chorus of voices chattering, and as they get closer, they quiet. I squeeze my eyes shut, then turn around and face the team.

Somehow, they all managed to arrive at the same time today,

because of course they did. I scan the group, my eyes landing on Mariah, Anh next to her, Trinity behind her. Mariah's head tilts and then her gaze lands on the mess at my feet.

"Here, I'll help you," Sherika says and steps forward. I kneel beside her, and we put all my things back into my bag.

"What happened?" One of the girls asks. Her name's Jaya, and she's one of Sherika's friends. "Are you OK, Hayley?"

We both straighten up, and I heft my pack onto my shoulder. I look Jaya in the eye. "I forgot my keys."

A collective groan rises from my teammates. I want to throw up or sink into the sidewalk and disappear.

"This has happened so many times," someone says.

"That's what we get for trusting a sophomore," someone else mutters.

"Hey!" Sherika says sharply, and they all go quiet. "It's just a mistake."

"Yeah, and it's, like, the fifth time she's made this mistake," Jaya says. "No offense, but we need a different keyholder."

I stare down at the ground while they debate back and forth. Jaya wants to tell Coach; Sherika says I could just give the keys to someone else. When they take a vote, almost everyone sides with Jaya—even Anh and Trinity raise their hands, mouthing a sorry at me. I shrug, swallowing my tears. Mariah doesn't vote at all.

"OK." Jaya looks at me. "It's nothing personal. But we need to be sure we can have practice when we planned it. This is serious for a lot of us."

"It's serious for me, too," I say, my voice cracking.

"Well." Jaya shrugs. She turns to the rest of the group. "Anyone want to come jog the track with me? We can at least do some footwork drills."

Sherika gives me a sympathetic look, then follows Jaya down toward the playfields with most of the team.

Mariah lingers. "You gonna join?"

I shake my head.

She sighs. "Hayley, what's going on with you? You're not getting into sketchy shit, are you?"

"No!" I rub my face. "No. It's dumb."

"It's not over some crush, is it?"

I don't reply.

"Oh my god." Mariah shakes her head. "Listen. I don't know who's got you down bad, but I know you love basketball, maybe more than a lot of the people here. And basketball won't break your heart. So figure it out, because I want you with me on the varsity team this year."

I nod.

Her expression softens. "You want a hug?"

I nod again.

She steps forward and wraps her arms around me. She smells like coconut oil, and her hug is brief but firm. She pulls back, resting a hand on my shoulder, and I make myself meet her eyes. They're deep brown and kind. "You got this."

"Thanks," I say, even though I don't feel like I've got it at all. She squeezes my shoulder once and walks away.

When I get home, I can hear Sam in the kitchen singing along to Olivia Rodrigo. Judging from the sounds, they're cooking or baking something. I wanted to bake, but I also want to be alone, so I head upstairs and send them a text to let them know I'm here.

In my room, I flop down on my bed and stare at the ceiling. The frustrated faces of my teammates fill my mind. I can't believe I'm letting my crush on Talia ruin our friendship and basketball, too. My vision blurs and tears slide down my temples. I roll onto my side, facing the wall, and curl up with my arms around my favorite stuffed animal. It's a velveteen cat. Dad won it for me at the state fair when I was a kid.

I cry quietly for a while, and eventually the tears peter out and I just lie there with my eyes closed. I'm too exhausted from everything that's happened in the past few days to really sob; it's like my emotions have flatlined.

My phone pings. I don't want to check it, but the hovering specter of the notification itches my brain until I roll over and fumble it out of my bag.

Hey, what's your address? It's Jaya. The team voted me key-holder, and I wanna get them tonight.

I text her the address, and she says she'll come by around six.

So that's it, I guess. I failed my friendship with Talia and I failed my responsibility as keyholder.

"Hayley?" It's Sam, tapping on my door. "You want a cupcake?"

"Sure," I say. "Come in." I don't really want to see anyone right now but a cupcake sounds nice.

The door opens, and they come in with a plate of pink-frosted chocolate cupcakes. "I didn't mix up the baking powder and baking soda this time," they say proudly.

I smile in spite of myself. When I got into baking a few years ago, before it became a de-stressing activity and was just a new hobby I was fixated on, Sam wanted to learn, too. The first time they baked, the cupcakes looked and tasted awful because of that mistake; that was also the last time they baked before today.

"What's the occasion?" I say, sitting up and grabbing one from the plate.

"You seemed down, and I wanted to cheer you up." They look at the plate, shifting from foot to foot.

"Sam." I'm tearing up again. "That's so sweet." I motion for them to sit down, and they do.

"How is it?" they ask, watching my face as I take the first bite. The cupcake is moist and light, with a rich chocolate flavor complemented by the sugary icing.

"Ohmahgaw," I mumble around the bite. "Issogood."

Sam beams. We eat our cupcakes in silence for a minute and finish at the same time, both of us reaching for another.

"So . . . what's going on?" Sam asks. "Mom wouldn't tell me . . . but I was in the hallway for a minute yesterday and I heard you say something about Talia." Their voice is light, too light. I know that means they were in the hallway for a lot longer than a minute—and probably happened to be right in front of my door the whole time. But I don't mind it, for some reason. It makes me feel like I matter.

So I tell Sam the truth, even though they probably overheard my whole conversation with Mom.

"Are you guys gonna be OK?" Sam chews on their lower lip.

My heart pangs. "I . . . don't know."

"Oh." Sam's mouth turns down and they gaze at me. "Have you talked to her since then?"

I shake my head. I know Sam's trying to help, and the cupcakes taste amazing, but this line of questioning is just making me feel worse.

"What if you just told her you had a panic attack?" Sam says. "It's partly true."

"Over what, though?" I ask. "How do I tell her that without telling her everything?"

Sam shrugs. "Just say you got overwhelmed by being on a double date and that the strategy's stressing you out."

I arch an eyebrow. "So lie to her?"

"I mean, it's kind of true," Sam says. "Right?"

"I guess." I take a deep breath. I don't want to leave Talia or anyone else hanging much longer; it feels like the window of time where I can go back to pretending everything is fine and normal is closing fast. I have to come up with something. And Sam is right. It's not the whole truth, but it's partly true.

The strategy is stressing me out, and the double date was over-whelming. I don't have to tell Talia it was because I have a giant crush on her.

OK. This sounds doable. Talia is probably too busy with Rose to even question it.

CHAPTER TWENTY

THE NEXT MORNING I lie in bed late, and I don't go to practice. Jaya picked up the keys last night, so it doesn't matter if I'm there or not. And by "picked up the keys," I mean I put them in our mailbox so she could grab them without me having to see her. I know I can't avoid my problems forever, but I can stretch it out as long as possible.

Eventually, when I'm sure my family is gone for the day, I go out on the back porch to eat some cereal and mindlessly scroll on socials for a bit. That's when my phone screen does that shift that means a phone call is incoming. A split-second later the name lights up my screen and makes my stomach lurch: Coach Kay.

I answer it.

"How's your morning, Hayley?" she asks.

"It's OK. I . . . didn't come to practice today."

"I know. I'm in my office right now."

"Oh."

I hear the shuffle of papers. "Jaya texted me yesterday and let me know what happened, so I thought I'd come down and make sure things were OK. I was surprised you aren't here."

I push my foot against the wooden boards of the back steps. "I'm sorry."

"You don't need to apologize. I'm worried about you. I know how much you love this sport and our team; you're one of the girls I count on to make it a welcoming atmosphere."

Tears sting my eyes and I blink. *Coach counts on me?*

"I know you might feel less important because you're JV," Coach continues. "But JV is the cocoon where caterpillars can take their time to grow, if you'll excuse the cheesy metaphor. That's where I learn who's got what skills and who needs what kind of nurturing to become the best player they can be. And I look for the team members who bring that out in others. Team members like you, Hayley."

"Thanks," I say, the word coming out way more tearful than I thought it would.

"What do you need, Hayley? I see your potential and I want to support you."

I swallow hard, trying not to let the sobs break out. "I feel like I let you down," I say. "Everyone thinks I'm a flake and hates me now."

"I don't believe that. They're frustrated, sure, but that's just because they count on you. You wanna know what some of the girls have said to me?" She doesn't wait for me to answer. "They've said, 'Hayley's always so reliable, I don't know what happened.' 'Hayley's never late.' 'Hayley cares about the team; that's why she started this practice group.'"

Tears are rolling down my cheeks now, and I swipe them away.

"They want you here; they're just confused. And they're worried we're going to lose a great teammate."

"I want to be on the team," I whisper.

"I know you do. So how can I help you with that?"

"It's just . . ." My voice is all wobbly now. I've never been emotional like this in front of Coach. "Keyholder is a big responsibility, and I wanted to do it—wanted to show I'm varsity material—but this summer has been really stressful, and it shouldn't even matter because it's just—"

I stop myself, the tears choking my words, which is probably good because I shouldn't tell Coach anyway. Then she really will think I'm irresponsible.

"Deep breath," Coach says, and we pause for a minute, taking breaths together over the phone. "I know you struggle with anxiety. But I want you to know that you don't have to do that to prove you're varsity material. Leadership qualities are important, but I don't need a team of leaders. I need a team of girls who know what they bring to the court and how that fits in with the others. And you bring compassion, a community-building ethic—and an unmatched three-pointer."

I laugh a little at that. "OK," I say. It's hard to believe I deserve all this praise, that Coach really sees it in me, but I've seen her when players talk back, so I'm not about to question her.

"I've decided that keyholder is too much pressure to place on one girl's shoulders," she says. "Jaya and Anh are going to be joint keyholders the rest of the summer so that they have backup, in case anything happens. And I just want you to show up and focus on bringing yourself to the court as a player, OK?"

I take a deep breath and blow it out. "I can do that."

"That's what I like to hear. I'll see you at the gym tomorrow morning."

We hang up and I shake out my limbs, letting all the shame and anxiety and dread out of my body. Knowing what Coach really thinks of me, knowing she noticed me before I ever formed this practice group, eases the knots in my stomach a little. I stand up and stretch, taking a deep breath of the fresh, earthy scent of the backyard. It rained during the night, and the air is cool but humid. My body wants to move. Maybe I'll go for a run.

When I get home an hour or so later, my mind is clear and my legs are pleasantly rubbery. I gulp cold water in the kitchen, then run upstairs for a quick shower to cool down.

Afterward, I sit on my bed and stare at my phone. I ran a different route than usual today so I wouldn't go past Talia's, but it's time to face my fears.

Kind of. I'm not going to tell them everything, but I am going to do what Sam suggested.

Hey, I text to the group chat. I'm sorry for leaving you all hanging. I had a really bad panic attack on Saturday. I got stressed out by the double date and the strategy, and I've just been avoiding everything ever since. I hope I didn't worry anyone too much.

I wait, staring at the screen, heart pounding. A few minutes later, Kev texts a heart emoji. We love you, just glad you're OK.

If you wanna talk about anything, we're here for you, Jacob adds.

Suddenly the screen changes and a split second later my phone rings. It's Bri. FaceTiming me. They never call me unprompted.

I squeeze my eyes shut and take a deep breath. Then I open them and answer the call.

"So what's really going on?" Bri asks.

I pull back. "What do you mean?"

"Hayley." They shake their head. I can see from their background that they're sitting at their desk, probably drawing as usual. "I have to ask you a question."

I look at them, and they gaze back, their eyebrows drawn together. I don't know how to say no without sounding super suspicious. "What?"

"Do you have a crush on Talia?"

I open my mouth, grasping for words, but I can't think of anything. As long as no one asked, I could hide it. Maybe not well, but I was doing OK. But now Bri's asking me, and I can't lie to their face. I can't even tell a half-truth, not that I can think of one.

"How did you know?" I ask quietly. My hands are shaking all of a sudden, and I prop the phone on my nightstand.

Bri looks down, nodding, then looks at me again. Their round face is serious, skin glowing in the sunlight reflecting off their desk. "I just put it together. When we talked about Talia having a crush you didn't know about, and then when you asked me not to tell her we talked about it, and then this . . ."

"I didn't even know it when I talked to you!" My voice sounds strangled, caught between a sob and a laugh.

Bri smirks, shaking their head. "I mean, I wasn't sure. But it seemed like the logical conclusion, and . . ." They spread their hands wide. "I was right."

My chest is tight, my stomach churning. "Please don't tell her."

"Of course not." Bri frowns. "You're the one who needs to do that."

"I can't."

"What? Why not?"

"She has Rose." Tears are in my eyes now, and I look away from Bri's gentle, confused gaze. "I want her to be happy and it'll be easier if I'm just . . ." I swallow. "Not around."

"What do you mean?" Bri sits up straight.

I shrug.

"Hayley. Talia loves you. You can't just dip out on her."

"She won't notice."

Bri bursts out laughing. "Are you serious? Do you know what the last three days have been like? We've been talking every day. She cries on the phone because she's scared for you and your mental health, and worried that she did something wrong. Sorry, but that half-ass text isn't enough. You need to talk to her. You've been friends since you were *literal babies*. She deserves the truth."

The force of Bri's words has me a little stunned. *If Bri saw through me, does everyone else think the same thing? I can't even argue, though, because they're right. My text was half-assed at best.*

"But what's the point?" I eventually say. "She doesn't like me back. Telling her is just going to make things more awkward."

Bri lifts an eyebrow. "Do you know how many times me and Kev and Jacob have wondered when you two are going to get together?"

"What?!"

"Yeah!" Bri throws their hands up. "Maybe she's just as oblivious to her feelings as you were, but I'd be very surprised if she rejects you."

My mind is racing. *This whole time our friends have been waiting for us to date? As if it's a sure thing? Bri sounds so certain.* "But Rose . . ."

"Fuck Rose!" Bri says impatiently. My jaw drops. Bri almost never curses, and they quickly press their hand against their mouth. "What I mean is . . . I'm sure Rose is nice, but they're not you. And Talia hasn't said a word about them this whole time. She's been talking about you. You need to tell her."

"I don't know," I say. "I need to think about this."

"OK," Bri says. "But I'm not going to let you mess up your friendship. Or our whole group dynamic."

"Ouch." I wrinkle my nose.

"I'm sorry." Bri takes a deep breath. "Am I coming on too strong?"

"No. I . . ." I take deep breaths, trying to calm myself. "You're good. It's just . . . it's all been a lot."

They grimace. "I know. I'm just . . . I'm worried about you, too." Their voice cracks.

"You are?"

"Hayley." They look at me, eyes serious. "We all love you. Like, so much. I want you to be happy, and I want Talia to be happy, and . . . I really think you could be happy together."

I wipe my eyes. Somehow my face is all wet. *Have I been crying this whole time?*

"I love you guys, too," I whisper.

"And I'm here for you," Bri says. "We all are. Whatever you need. You don't have to shut us out. Or Talia. It's like you told me: the door's open; you just need to walk through it. The door may not be open in the way you want, but it's definitely not closed yet."

I pull up the neckline of my shirt and dry off my face. "Way to use my own words against me. Again."

They snicker. "It's not my fault you give good advice."

I can't help but smile. "OK. I'll think about it."

"I'll take that." They gaze at me. "You gonna be all right?"

I nod, even though I'm not at all sure if that's true, and then we hang up.

It takes me a long time to fall asleep that night. I can't stop thinking about what Bri said and playing out different scenarios in my head about how to tell Talia my feelings. When I finally do drift off, I'm in and out of fuzzy dreams all night and wake up with anxiety buzzing in my chest.

The anxiety gets worse on my bus ride to practice. As I walk up toward the gym, I see my teammates filtering in, and I have to stop under a tree at the far edge of the field to steady myself. Pulling out my water bottle, I take a long drink of water, the melting ice cubes clinking inside.

I take a deep breath. The air is fresh and mildly sweet, and the sky is perfectly clear and sunny.

I can do this.

I step out from under the shade of the branches and head toward the gym again. At the door, I pause for a minute, then pull it open and walk inside.

Sneakers screech on the floor as girls dribble and drive into the basket to shoot in turns. Everyone's warming up, so no one notices me come in. Pop music blasts from the speakers. I set my bag down on the sidelines and do some jumping jacks, as much to shake off my anxiety as to loosen my muscles.

"Hayley!" I turn and see Mariah heading toward me with a big grin on her face. "You're back."

"I'm back," I say, striking a pose way more confident than I feel inside.

"How are you?" she asks, and I know what she's really asking. I lower my arms. "I'm . . . OK. Still stressed about stuff."

"Your crush?"

I nod.

"Girl, who is it?"

"It's . . ." I hesitate, but it's not like Mariah is friends with my friends. "Talia."

Her eyes widen. "Your bestie?"

"Yeah."

"Oh shit." She laughs. "Well, I get why you've been so caught up in it." Then her eyes soften. "Seriously, though. I'm glad you're back. It's not the same without you. You wanna warm up with me?"

I nod and follow her out onto the court, catching the ball she tosses to me. We take turns going for layups and rebounding each other's shot. A couple girls glance at me and whisper to each other. My shoulders stiffen, and I miss a three-pointer I'd usually make. I can feel eyes on me and part of me wants to run out of the gym, but I don't.

I pass the ball to Mariah, then guard her all the way to the hoop. She makes her shot, and I collect the ball. And when Jaya and Sherika call the girls to center court, I stand in the back, focusing on my breathing and their words as they lay out the plan for the morning. People are obviously still annoyed at me. It's fine, though. I can handle this.

I can.

I think.

CHAPTER TWENTY-ONE

I TRY TO DO what Bri suggested. I really do. On the bus home that day, I take deep breaths, trying to stay present. *Talia's my best friend. She wants to hear from me.*

I get off the bus a stop early to go talk to her. The neighborhood is hazy and still under the hot midday sun. Everything is lush and green, bees humming in the flowery shrubs that line the street to Talia's. My heart pounds. My stomach turns. I can smell my own sweat, and it's not regular basketball practice sweat. It's anxiety sweat, rank and sharp.

Everything Bri said last night feels distant now. *What if they're wrong? What if Talia isn't just worried about me—what if she's mad now?*

I take one step at a time, until her house comes into view at the end of the block, then I stop. My breathing is shallow. *Am I going to faint?* I reach out a hand and grab the fence next to me. This was a mistake.

I backtrack as fast as I can and go down a block to avoid her house entirely.

The next morning, I decide to try again. Going to see her in person is clearly too much for me, so when I get to the gym for practice, I go into the bathroom, lock myself in a stall, and stare down at my phone, willing myself to open her text messages. I can hear the distant thuds of basketballs hitting the gym floor, the chaotic rhythm matching my heartbeat. My finger hovers over the message icon on my screen.

Come on. Just one tap.

There.

The thread opens up and fills the screen—and then panic fills my chest and I exit the app and then the bathroom, striding across the court and stuffing my phone all the way into the bottom of my backpack.

By Friday, I still haven't talked to Talia, and she stopped trying to text and call me. She never responded to the message I sent to the group, and any hope I had that my half-ass effort would smooth things over has shrunk to nothing.

Somehow, though, I can't get myself to do anything about it. Every time I pick up my phone, telling myself this time I'll text her, I freeze and swipe away—to social media, one of the games on my phone, literally anything else.

I'm waiting for the bus back home from practice when my phone pings.

PARTY TIME, Kev says in the group chat.

What is he talking about?

Hayley you're our hookup. He texts again a moment later. What time should we meet up? Where is it?

Oh.

Oh no.

It's the beginning of August, and my teammate's party is tonight. I didn't hear anyone mention it at practice, but the second I think it, my phone pings some more, the team chats lighting up with the address and time. I don't want to go. All I want to do is curl up in bed and lose myself in TV until I forget that I'm probably destroying one of the most important relationships in my life.

Jacob texts a string of celebration emojis. My friends have all been looking forward to this party, and I can't let them down again. The thought of that feels even worse than going to the party.

I text them Victoria's address. I'm so ready!!!!!!!! I say, and immediately cringe. Even for me, that's a lot of exclamation points. I picture Bri on the other end of this chat, seeing right through my fake excitement.

Me and Bri are coming together, Jacob says.

Imma just walk, Kev says. Talia and Hayley, you wanna walk with me?

My mom's going to drop me off, Talia says, and my heart jolts at the sight of her profile picture in the chat. She doesn't say anything else, but the message is clear: she doesn't want anything to do with me.

It's Family Fun Friday, so I won't be able to get down there until we're done, I say. I'll let Victoria know you're coming. See you there!

Everyone but Talia reacts with a heart or thumbs up. The bus rolls up and I get on, swallowing over and over so I won't cry.

I'm dreading the party, so of course the evening goes by way too fast. Dinner is a blur, and even the action movie we watch can't distract me from the pit of anxiety churning in my stomach. As the credits roll, my phone lights up with texts from my friends as they arrive at the party.

I make my way upstairs and stand frozen in front of my open closet. *Maybe I can say I have a headache or something.*

I check my phone and see a text from Bri, just to me. You on your way yet? I look at the message for way too long, and it's like they're psychic, because a few minutes later they text me again: You ARE still coming, right? Talia's here. You should talk to her. I think it would help.

I don't believe that at all, but I'm clearly not getting out of this that easily, so I respond. Yeah, I'm coming. Just getting ready.

I choose my favorite sundress; it's the color of an orange creamsicle, with a high neck, a fitted waist, and a flared skirt. I accessorize it with big glittery hoops and my white Birkenstocks, do my eyeliner, and tie a fanny pack and a flannel around my waist. It's warm now, but even summer nights can get cool in Seattle.

I put in my earbuds and listen to music on the walk down, taking deep breaths of the evening air as I make my way toward Lake Washington, where Victoria's house is. The sun is just starting to set behind me, and the warm breeze ruffles my hair. I slow my stride as I head down the hill into Madison Valley, fighting the urge to turn back. I pass Café Flora, blinking back the tears that well up, and then I'm out of the business strip and turning off into the neighborhood that runs south along the lake. Here, the houses shift into an array of different mansions: big stately brick homes, modern boxes on boxes, buildings that look like they should be in the French countryside instead of Seattle. The street is wide, with tall broad-limbed trees spreading above me.

Victoria lives in a brick house a few blocks in. I stand and stare up at it; the house is three floors with a stained-glass window sparkling where the roof comes to a point above the front door, and it has a massive yard that's surrounded by a tall fence with a vine-covered arbor over the gate.

As I enter and the gate clicks shut behind me, I hear the sound of laughter and music drifting from behind the house. The front yard is landscaped with so many bushes, vines, and trees that it feels like being in a forest. I follow the cobblestone path through the garden, around the side of the house, and into the backyard.

Green grass stretches down to the back fence, with a view of the Cascade mountains across the lake. My teammates and their friends mill everywhere: Jude and their girlfriend, Katie, are sitting with their friends around the koi pond at one corner, Sherika and Jaya are playing badminton at the net set up in another corner, and others are hanging out at the long tables clearly brought out for this purpose. The grill is going, overseen by a red-haired man I assume is Victoria's dad. He's directing a couple of the girls' boyfriends in the proper way to grill burgers, and there's Bri in the midst of them, nodding along. *Of course. They love learning new things.* Karina stands beside them.

I walk up behind the two of them and tap Bri on the shoulder. They jump and turn, breaking into a huge grin when they see me.

"You came!" They throw their arms around me.

"Good to see you, buddy." Karina grins at me.

I force a smile and give them both a thumbs up. "I'm here! Let's party!"

Bri squints at me, and I can tell they want to ask me more, but Karina's here, so they just eye me. "Talia's playing croquet with Jacob and Kevin and some of their chess club buddies." They point, and I follow the line of their finger down to the edge of the lawn.

And there she is.

Talia is tanned and glowing, like she is by this time every summer, with her dark curls loose around her face. She's wearing an emerald green striped tank top and black denim shorts that hug her figure. *When did I start noticing her figure?* But now I am, and I can't take my eyes off the curve of her hips, her slim shoulders. *She's so pretty.*

"I'm gonna get a LaCroix," I say to Bri and Karina and dart away before they can reply. It's all too much: the way Bri looks at me with sympathy, the feeling in my chest, seeing Talia after avoiding her for a week. We've never gone this long without seeing each other unless one of us was on a family vacation. I don't know what to say to her. And I'm worried if I'm alone with her, I'll tell her everything, and I'm not ready yet. *Maybe later.*

Maybe.

Near the open patio doors that lead into the house, I spot two stainless steel patio coolers with a sign pasted above them: DRINKS HERE.

I open one and scan the array of seltzer waters and soda inside. It's almost too many choices, but I know what I want. I grab a key lime LaCroix, crack it open, and close the cooler.

Thank god there isn't alcohol at this party. I've never been to a party where that was happening, though I've heard stories from the older players on our bus rides to away games. None of my friends or I drink, and I'm fine with that. It's too easy to picture what would happen if I got drunk. Goodbye what little filter I have; hello spilling my feelings all over Talia.

"Hayley!" Arms encircle me. I recognize Mariah's voice as she gives me a tight squeeze.

I turn around, smiling at her. "What's up?"

"I see you brought . . ." She lowers her voice but jerks her head back not-so-subtly.

"I didn't bring her. We all came separately."

She raises her eyebrows. "Everything OK?"

I give her the TL;DR of my panic attack, and she shakes her head. "It really hasn't been your week, huh."

"Yeah." I can feel the tears welling in my eyes, the lump swelling in my throat. "I feel like I'm messing everything up. With the team, too."

"Hey." She puts a hand on my arm, her kind eyes holding mine. "Everything's gonna be OK. The team is cool with you."

"It didn't seem like it at practice," I choke out.

She sighs. "OK, yeah, some of them are petty bitches, but that's on them. I was just worried about you, and I know a lot of the players are glad you're back. They were annoyed by the lateness, but they're over it now."

I take a deep breath. I know she's right. Nobody's given me any weird looks yet tonight. Maybe it's not as big a deal as I thought it was. "Thanks."

"I got you," she says. "Wanna come see the tree house?"

My eyes widen. "Hell yeah."

We leave the patio, walking right past Talia's croquet game. As I pass, she glances over and our eyes lock. She opens her mouth, stepping toward me, but I look away and hurry after Mariah. My nose stings and I swallow the tears down. I'm such a coward.

The tree house sits in a massive oak tree at the end of the lawn. It's a far cry from the basic plywood shelter my dad built in our backyard when we were little.

This tree house has multiple entrances and exits: a rope you can slide down, a ladder fixed to one end, and a narrow staircase that winds up around the trunk. The house itself is built around the center of the trunk, where the main branches split and spread out over the lawn. It's not a square; I can't tell how many sides there are, but definitely more than four. The roof is conical and shingled, with a tiny carved weather vane on top. I can see a few people up in the house through the tiny windows sprinkled around the outside.

"They did not fuck around," I say, and Mariah laughs. I follow her up the staircase, clinging to the banister that's fixed to the tree.

The door at the top is small, and we have to crawl on our hands and knees. Inside, the tree house is surprisingly spacious, though currently filled up by people sitting around in a circle.

"We're playing Never Have I Ever!" one of the girls says. "Wanna join?"

We nod, and everyone squeezes down to make room for us. Across from us, Jaya and Sherika wave at me, and I wave back. And for the first time in a while, I feel my shoulders relax, just a little bit.

CHAPTER TWENTY-TWO

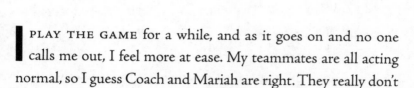

I PLAY THE GAME for a while, and as it goes on and no one calls me out, I feel more at ease. My teammates are all acting normal, so I guess Coach and Mariah are right. They really don't hate me. It's not the end of the world that I messed up.

Eventually I get bored and slip out of the tree house while they're all laughing about someone admitting to eating their own boogers. We're on the east side of Capitol Hill, and the sun has vanished behind it now, the sky turning a deep blue as evening approaches. The lights strung on the arbor above the patio are on, casting a magical golden glow over the kids eating burgers at the tables. My stomach growls.

Maybe I can talk to Talia tonight after all. But first, I need some food.

Bri's flipping burgers at the grill, with Victoria's dad overseeing. They look up and smile as I approach. "Look at this! You can call me grillmaster now!"

"They're a natural," Victoria's dad says. "I gotta hit the bathroom. You got this?"

"Oh yeah," Bri says, waving him away.

I grab a paper plate and bun from the table beside the grill, loading up with toppings: pickles, bell peppers, lettuce, mayo, mustard, ketchup. Bri plops a burger on top of all of it, then deposits the remaining patties onto another plate. They fix up their own burger as I stand there chomping on mine.

"So have you talked to her yet?" They narrow their eyes at me.

I shake my head. "I'm going to, though," I say through a mouthful. "I promise."

They pause, staring at me. "Really?"

I nod, even though I don't feel half as sure as I sound. I already wish I hadn't said anything. The comfort of Mariah's pep talk and the tree house vibes are wearing off, and the anxiety is coming back.

"Well, here's your chance." Bri lifts a hand in the direction of the house. Talia's at the drink coolers, her back to me. "She ended things with Rose, by the way."

The back of my neck prickles. *No more Rose. Just me and Talia, both single. If this were a movie, this would be the moment everything comes to a head. We'd talk and cry and fall into each other's arms. And maybe even kiss.*

"I'll hold your food," Bri says, already reaching for my plate. I let them take it.

I can't walk this back now. If I can make it through letting down my teammates, then I should be able to talk to my best friend.

I take a deep breath and head toward Talia, the noise of the party fading as I focus on her.

She shuts the cooler as I come up, turning with a drink in her hand and stepping toward me at the same time. Our eyes meet and she freezes.

So do I.

I did *not* think this through.

"Hey," I blurt out.

She stares at me, clutching the can close to her chest. We stand there for what feels like minutes.

"Can we talk?" I ask, because I don't know where to start.

She nods.

"Um. OK. I was just wondering. Are we OK?"

"Are we OK." Her voice is flat and her forehead sinks into a frown.

"Yeah. Um. I texted the group to explain what happened after the panic attack, and you didn't respond."

She lets out a breath slowly. "I just . . . don't understand why you didn't tell me that before. Why you told the whole group and didn't text me first. I called and texted you a million times right after the date, but you didn't respond."

"I know." I'm grasping for words, but they aren't coming. I know I need to tell her the whole truth, but I don't know how, especially here, in front of all these people. I'm sweating. *Maybe they're all staring at us right now, watching us break down. Are we breaking down? Is this it for our friendship?* "I'm sorry."

"What happened?" Her voice cracks. "I thought we were best friends."

"We are!" I say. If she cries, I'll cry. The words are right there in the back of my throat, but I can't force them out.

She sets down her can on top of the fridge, flexing her hands, then flapping them. She's getting overloaded. "A best friend wouldn't—wouldn't—wouldn't—" She flaps faster and then whirls, striding away from me around the corner of the house.

I follow her, dodging around groups of kids chattering in the spaces between the tables. Talia's moving quickly, already around the side of the house now. It's not as well-lit here; there are tiny solar lamps along the footpath, but all they really show me is my feet as I speedwalk after her. I can see her shadow disappearing around the front of the house, and I break into a jog, almost stumbling on a tree root.

The front gate clicks closed, and I pull it open. Talia's on her phone, the blue light making her face glow. The street is still and quiet; we're the only ones out here.

"Talia," I say.

She looks up. There are tears on her cheeks. "What?!" she snaps.

Her tone is a bolt to my chest. "Where are you going?"

"Home." She looks down at her phone again and taps the screen a few times.

"Why?"

"Are you serious?" She whirls to face me head-on. "You ig-nore me for a week, you avoid me for this entire party—" her voice breaks. "Bri said you liked me!"

Oh. Of course. Bri said they wouldn't tell Talia, but they did. My heart sinks.

"And the thing is, I . . ." She presses her hands to her eyes. "I like you, too! I've known it since I figured out I'm demi! You're the second person I've ever had a crush on."

Oh my god.

It was me.

I was the second crush. Just like that, my heart is lifting, like it's on the most dramatic roller coaster ever. *Talia liked me this whole time, before I even knew my own feelings. I can't believe it.*

She barrels on. "And I thought maybe you liked me, too, but then you told me to go after Rose and I thought for sure you didn't. So I tried to give them a chance, but all I could think about this whole week was you and our friendship and whether you were OK, and how I wanted to just come over and hold you and never let go—" She's sobbing now.

"Bri was right," I say, reaching both hands out to her, but she doesn't close the gap. "I do like you! But I didn't want to ruin our friendship, so I thought if you went out with Rose again, you'd get together with them and then I could get rid of my crush, and everything would be OK!"

"Oh my god." She squeezes her hands into fists at her sides. "You—that's why you wanted me to go out with Rose?! For your own benefit?"

"No!" I'm crying now, too. "I didn't mean it that way! I just wanted you to be happy. I like you so much, Talia, please."

"That's not enough," she chokes out and then she folds over into a crouch, gripping her hair with her hands.

"I'm sorry," I sob, crouching beside her, reaching out to her again.

"Don't touch me!" She snaps, and I yank it back. "Meltdown."

"OK. OK. I won't touch you." I look wildly around. Talia's melted down in front of me before, but never on a dark street in a neighborhood we don't know. I could scream for help, but that might make her sensory overwhelm even worse. I could run into the backyard and get someone, but I don't want to leave her alone. I don't want to mess this up even more than I already have.

A car pulls up, and my heart flips for a second, but then I recognize it. Her mom steps out. "Sweetie?"

Talia makes a wordless noise and her mom strides over, kneeling beside her, talking to her in a quiet voice. After a moment, Talia nods. Her mom guides her upright, hands on her shoulders, then directs her to the passenger side. I'm frozen, unable to do or say anything. She opens the door and I watch as Talia disappears into the front seat.

Her mom buckles her in and shuts the door. "What happened? Are you girls OK?"

"We . . ." I don't know what to say.

"Did you have a fight?" Her mom's face softens.

I nod, because it's the easiest thing to do. I can feel the tears rolling down my cheeks.

"I'm going to call your parents, OK, honey?" she says. "You just go back inside the gate and wait until they get here."

I nod again, because there's nothing else I can do. I've never had a fight with Talia before. This is our first one, and it feels like the end of everything, like I've actually ruined our friendship.

I go back inside the yard and slump on the front step. A few minutes later, I hear Talia's car pull away. Then the street is silent again. And I'm alone. People laugh in the backyard, but it's muffled. I stare down at the front walk. My face is wet from tears, but I can't summon the energy to wipe them away.

My phone pings. *Oh right. My phone.*

On my way, Mom says. Stay where you are.

I couldn't move if I wanted to. All the adrenaline and panic are draining from my body, leaving me feeling like a lead weight.

A stick cracks, and I startle, scanning the darkness on either side of the house.

"It's me." Bri steps out from the side of the house.

I stare at them as they edge into the glow of the porch light. They fidget nervously with their hands, cracking their knuckles and flexing their fingers over and over.

"I'm so sorry. I heard everything," they say. "I followed you because I was worried, but then I figured ... I didn't want to interrupt."

Anger roars to life in my chest. "Yeah, I think you've done enough," I snap, and their head jerks back slightly.

"I'm sorry," they whisper.

"It's too fucking late for that." My voice cracks as fresh tears roll down my face. "I can't believe you told her."

"I know. I'm sorry. It just kind of came out. We were talking, and she was so upset and then she told me, and I—I didn't think. I was worried you were going to keep ignoring things, and if she knew, then she could talk to you and everything would be OK again—"

"This isn't about you!" I stand up, and they step back. "You're always so concerned about our friend group, but I'm part of the group, too! This wasn't your secret to tell!"

"I know," they say, voice pleading.

"Hayley?"

We both turn to the gate. My mom is standing there, silhouetted by the streetlights.

"I think it's time to go, honey," she says softly, and that's all I need. I stride past Bri, not even looking at them, and out toward our car idling at the curb. A moment later, Mom gets in from the driver's side, and we pull away. She doesn't say anything, just puts her hand on my knee.

I reach out and curl my hand around hers. As we leave the neighborhood, my chest cracks open, the numbness gone and the pain filling my body, and I sob all the way home.

I spend the weekend in bed. Talia doesn't text me. Neither does Bri. Which is good, because Bri's the last person I want to hear from. *If it wasn't for them pushing me to talk to Talia, maybe we wouldn't have fought. If my friends hadn't forced me to come to the party, if Bri had just kept their mouth shut, if . . .*

If I'd just been honest with Talia to begin with.

Talia likes me back. Or liked me. I have no idea if she still does.

If I'd only said something earlier, everything would have worked out. We'd be holding hands right now instead of fighting.

I watch episode after episode of cartoons, trying to think about literally anything else. My eyes are fixed on the screen, but all I can see are memories of my friendship with Talia, all the moments that shine differently in this new light now. The way she smiled at me and held my gaze whenever we talked. The way I couldn't help but notice what she wore every time I saw her. The way she's always been down for whatever wild scheme I've come up with, and the way she's come up with her own, sometimes just because of me—like the summer love strategy.

Did she like me then? Did I like her? Does it matter if neither of us knew about our own feelings?

I keep hearing her words in my head over and over: *"That's not enough."*

She's right. My feelings for her don't erase the pain I caused her. I can't hide behind my fear forever and let what happened in sixth grade rule my life. There's more to being in a relationship than I thought when we started all this; Bri and Karina showed me that. Feelings aren't always enough.

I need to put in the work.

And Talia's not the only person I need to apologize to. Maybe it's a small thing, but it's been weighing on me the way I treated Brenna at our date. I don't have her number, and I definitely don't have Rose's, and I can't exactly ask Talia, so I search through socials instead. I find Rose on Talia's follower list, and through Rose, I find Brenna.

Hey, I write. I wanted to say sorry for the way I acted on our date. I was totally checked out, but it wasn't because of you. I have feelings for Talia, and I was trying to hide them and not handling it well, so I panicked and ran out on all of you, which wasn't cool. You're really awesome though, and I hope you find someone amazing.

I send the DM.

My phone pings. There's a heart reaction on my message, and a minute later a reply pops up. Hey, it's cool! I wasn't hurt, I was just kind of worried and hoped you were OK. If you ever wanna just hang as friends sometime, let me know.

I heart react back. I could see that, actually.

That night, I sleep better than I have in a while. Nothing's really fixed, but I did something I can be proud of and that's enough right now.

On Sunday evening, I hear a soft knock on my door. When I grunt, my mom opens it and peeks through.

"Hi, honey. How you doing?"

I shrug. I'd managed to tell her the full story when we got home Friday night and sobbed for hours while she rubbed my back and said reassuring things that I can't really remember now.

"Do you feel up to seeing someone?"

I sit up. "Who is it?"

"Bri."

For a minute, I want to say no. Want to send them away, burrow deeper into my bed, and never come out.

But I'm tired of running from my life. I maybe—probably—definitely fucked things up with Talia already. I don't have to fuck them up with the rest of my friends.

"Sure," I say. "I gotta put on pants. Can you tell them I'll meet them on the porch?"

She nods, a small smile brightening her eyes. "You got it."

When she's gone, I slide out of bed and grab my sweats. First one leg, then the other. I take a deep breath, then head downstairs.

When I step outside, Bri stands up from the bench on our front porch. It's well past sunset, and mosquitoes are circling the porch lights. I take a step toward them, and behind me, the screen door clicks as it swings back into place. My bare feet are steady on the cool hardwood.

"Hey," Bri says, their voice quieter than usual.

"Hi."

We stand looking at each other, at least for as long as two neurodivergent people can. After a few seconds, we both look away, me at the mosquitoes bouncing off the lamp glass, them at the fidget toy in their hands.

"I'm really sorry," they say after a moment. "You're right. I was worried about you, but I was also worried about our group. And I shouldn't have told Talia about your crush."

"Thanks," I say. Without warning, tears well up, and when I speak again, my voice is ragged. "I also wish . . . I wish I'd listened to you and talked to Talia."

They laugh, and I can hear by the watery sound of it that they're starting to cry, too. "Maybe we can both be right."

"Yeah." I sneak a glance at them and am surprised to see them looking at me. Their eyes are hesitant but full of love. I know what they said is true. Maybe they didn't go about it the best way, but they care about me and Talia. And our friends.

"Can I hug you?" I ask, and they nod, stepping forward until we've got our arms wrapped tight around each other in the warm night.

After a minute, they give me a squeeze and we let go.

"You wanna . . . ?" They motion at the bench, and I nod. We both sit, looking out at the quiet street and the houses across from us, their windows glowing softly.

It feels almost too easy, that we could both apologize and have everything be OK again, just like that. But maybe that's how it should be. Maybe all the trust I've built with my friends over time—telling them about the things I'm fixated on instead of hiding them, letting out my bubbly energetic side and never being told that I'm too much, asking them for help navigating my crushes instead of relying only on Talia—maybe this is the payoff. It's not just me and Talia against the world.

I have more friends now, and even though we're not romantic, they all fit the qualities on my summer love strategy list, too. Funny. Encouraging. Easy to be around. Fun to talk to. Values friendship. Likes me for who I am. And one more: will reach out to me when I'm struggling.

Talia fits all those things, too, and so much more that I can't even put into words. I want to hold her hand. I want to kiss her. I want to make her happy. I feel like my heart is going to explode when I think about her. Crush feelings. And the other feelings too: a depth, a solidity, a calmness that could be love. Real love.

The person I was looking for was right in front of me all along. And when I think about it . . . I fit my own list, too. Or at least, I could. I just need to reach out to Talia. We're both struggling and maybe I can't fix it, but I can at least try.

I take a deep breath and turn to face Bri. "I want to tell Talia. I mean, I know she already knows. But I want to do it right, the way I should have. And apologize."

"We could go now," Bri says, shifting like they're going to stand up.

"No, no," I say, and it's not avoidance behind my words. Well, maybe a little. But it's more than that. "I want to tell her the way she deserves to be told. I want her to feel . . ." My throat closes up and I swallow, blinking back tears. Bri takes my hand. "I want her to feel how special she is to me." I smile at Bri. "I think there's one more step in the summer love strategy. Will you help me?"

CHAPTER TWENTY-THREE

W HAT I WANT to do takes a little while to coordinate. I have to find a day that week that Jacob, Kev, and Bri are all available, and then they have to talk to Talia without letting her know that something's up. Thursday evening is the only time we're all free, so I suffer through four basketball practices, two family dinners, and continued silence with Talia.

Well, except for one text.

I know I hurt her when I pulled away. At the time, it felt like the only thing I could do, but now that I might have lost our friendship for real, now that I'm not in the grip of the anxiety monster, I can see how wrong I was. The way I ignored her frantic calls and texts, tried to pass off my panic attack with a half-truth, avoided her at the party—remembering it makes my skin crawl.

I'm not doing that again.

So on Tuesday after dinner, I sit on my bed composing and revising texts over and over in my Notes app. None of them sound right. They're too formal, or too long, or too explain-y. I don't need to do that now. All I need is for her to know I'm not pulling away this time. I'm not going to ghost her. I'm here, and I want to fix this.

Finally, I take a deep breath, switch over to my texts, and just write from the heart.

I'm really sorry for what I did. I want to make it right. You don't have to text me back. I just wanted you to know I'm thinking about it, and I'm not going anywhere.

I stare at the thread for a few minutes. I don't know what I'm waiting for. She has read receipts off, so I don't even know if she's seen it. But I miss her so much, and I wish more than anything that I could go back in time and be brave. I know there were reasons why I was scared, but they were also in the past. This is the present. And I know who Talia is: She's my best friend, and even if we date and it doesn't work out in the end, I know we'll make it through.

At least, we will, if she wants to fix this, too.

On Thursday, I give myself plenty of time to prepare. I dress in my favorite short-sleeved crewneck crop-top with a giant sunflower pattern on it, high-waisted shorts, and my pink sandals. I pack my bag carefully; I don't want to forget anything. Mom helps me double-check, and then we're off. Talia never texted back, so maybe she won't even show up, but I have to try anyway.

The sun is just starting to set, turning trees and sidewalks to gold in its warm rays. The streets of Seattle feel enchanted in this moment. Hip-hop spills from a passing car, and someone at a bus stop busts a move to the beat; everyone on the sidewalk is laughing with their friends or walking like they're headed somewhere important. The breeze is warm, the trees lush and green, and a bubble of calm embraces me as we rattle over the Montlake bridge and pass between Husky Stadium and the University of Washington campus.

The drive into Magnuson Park is crowded, with cars parked illegally along the road toward the beach. It's not the hottest day this summer, but it's still mid-eighties, and when it's warm, people want to be near Lake Washington.

Just as we get to the end of the lot, Mom stops, and a car backs out of a spot in front of us.

"The parking gods have blessed us today," she says, slipping in as they drive away.

Looking out at the water and at the Cascade mountains, light blue with gold crests against the pink horizon, I take a deep breath. *I can do this.*

"If anything goes off the rails, I'll be right here," Mom says.

"Thank you." I look at her, and she smiles, her eyes misty.

"I'm so proud of you," she says.

I smile. She opens her arms, and I lean into her for a hug. We stay like that for a long moment, and then I pull away and get out of the car.

"Don't forget your backpack!" Mom calls as I start to shut the door. Of course. I almost left my bag sitting in the backseat.

Hefting it onto my shoulder, I walk southward down the path along the lake, away from the spot where we all went swimming at the beginning of the summer. I want somewhere a little more secluded; screaming children, barbecue smoke, and other people's music aren't the vibe right now.

The crowds peter out as I walk farther, until there's just a few pairs and small groups here and there on the grass. The air is a little hazy, with a faint sweet smell; wildfire season is starting.

Finally I spot a tall, pretty tree, its branches sweeping out over the water. There's no one under it, and the nearest people aren't too close. *Perfect.*

I open my bag and start to set everything up. First I lay out the huge pink fleece blanket from my bed, and the dinner plate wrapped up inside it goes on top, in the center. Then the electric tea lights around the edge; there's still plenty of light to see by, but the effect is important. And the effort. Then the Tupperware with our favorite cupcakes inside. I put them each on the dinner plate. Maybe her favorite flavor has changed without me knowing, but that's OK. What I know right now is this: her favorite is chocolate, with coffee-flavored frosting. Mine is vanilla, with chocolate frosting. The crowning touch is a pair of ice-cold key lime LaCroix. Can't forget the Skittle water.

I text my friends and settle in. Now all I have to do is wait.

Time slows way down as I sit there. The nerves are creeping in now, the bubble of calm dissipating. I know this is the right thing to do, but still. I've never put myself out there like this before. And if Talia says no after all this . . . well, of course she can. I don't want her to do anything she doesn't want to do. I'm just not sure how we'll come back from that.

But no matter what, I know I've tried. Avoiding what I'm afraid of doesn't solve anything. And if I'm going to put myself out there, Talia is the person I'd most want to do that for.

An image pops into my head: Talia and me, nine years old, splashing in water while our parents lounge in the grass watching us. Where were Sam and Ella? Somewhere, I'm sure. Sam would have been six? Seven? Ella was probably in middle school. In that moment, though, it was just me and Talia. We'd been reading a book series about animals, and we were pretending to be otters, playing in the shallows.

There's nothing else to the memory. Just the same calm happiness I always feel with her. Like she really gets me, loves me, thinks I'm cool. Like I'm safe with her.

Safe, like the time she yelled at some Bible-thumper who got in my face at our first Pride. He was standing in the middle of the sidewalk with one of those huge hateful signs they always carry, yelling at people passing by. I don't even remember what he said, just his contorted face in front of mine all of a sudden, and then Talia screaming right back. And her eyes, dark and on fire with indignation. Her hand squeezing mine. Her voice listing off all the logical fallacies of right-wing Christianity as she towed me away from him through the crowd.

She's always been there for me. And I've always been there for her. In middle school, her parents struggled with their marriage for a while. We had only come out to each other at that point, and she was afraid telling her parents would make things worse. There were so many nights she cried to me: about the puberty changes she hated, about the fights her parents were having, about her fear of the future if nothing changed—or if everything did. Her parents started couples counseling, and I came out to mine, and then she told hers, and it was like her murky gray world got its color back.

I've always been there for her.

Until now.

But I'm going to change that. I want to be the friend she deserves—and maybe even the girlfriend, too. If that's what she wants.

When my phone pings, a jolt of anxiety zips through my chest.

We're here, Kev says.

I stand up, scanning the path, looking for my friends in the current of people strolling up and down the lake. There are families walking past me back toward the beach area, parents laden with coolers and chairs, people on Rollerblades, older couples holding hands, gaggles of kids my age chattering and teasing each other. And—*there.*

Talia's talking to Bri and Jacob. Kev is right behind them, scanning the shoreline. His eyes finally land on me and light up, and I smile.

I look back at Talia, tall and gorgeous in a mustard yellow fit-and-flare sundress with cap sleeves. She looks up, away from

Bri, and I can tell they're all catching sight of me but all I can see is Talia.

Her eyes go wide and she stops. My friends stop, too, standing at the edge of the path, twenty feet of dry summer grass between us. Talia turns to Bri.

"What is this?" She sounds confused. Maybe upset. I can't tell.

"Hayley has something to tell you," Bri says.

"Were you all in on this?" Talia asks.

Kev and Jacob nod.

Talia turns back to me, mouth opening, then closing, like she wants to say something but can't find the words.

"Come sit with me," I say. "Please?"

She takes a step forward, then another, and slowly crosses the grass to the blanket. Her gaze sweeps over the cupcakes, the LaCroix, the tea lights, everything I laid out.

"You didn't have to do this," she says.

"I wanted to," I say. I look over her shoulder briefly; our friends are fading back into the crowd, heading up toward the beach.

When I look back at Talia, her eyes are full of tears.

"Why?" she chokes out.

"I'm really, really sorry," I say. "When I realized I like you, I panicked. You're my best friend, and I've never had a relationship, and I've always—" I'm choking up now, too, tears spilling over. "I was afraid. Ever since sixth grade. I've always been afraid. Back then it was because of homophobia and shit, you know, this whole dumpster fire society"—I wave my hand—"and everything I'd internalized. But after that it was just easier. If I never put myself out there, then I'd never be rejected, homophobically or otherwise." Now I'm really crying, and tears are streaming down Talia's face, too. "And then we made this plan, and we went to that concert, and I realized I was in love with you—" *Shit. I said The Thing.* "And—and I just freaked out because if I told you and you didn't like me, it would make everything awkward and I'd ruin our friendship, and maybe lose our whole friend group, and I've never had friends like all of you—it was just me and you for so long—and I thought it would be easier to hide it and make it go away, but I couldn't. I'm so sorry. I'm sorry I didn't tell you, and I'm sorry I pushed you toward Rose. And I'm sorry I shut you out. I should have treated you better because you deserve it, and I understand if you don't want to be with me and don't want to be my friend—"

"Stop," Talia sobs.

I shut my mouth, staring at her. She sits down heavily on the blanket, pressing her hands to her face. I sit, too, and wait, forcing myself to breathe, in and out, slow exhales.

"It hurt. *So much.*" She stares at my midsection, and I know it's the closest she can get to eye contact right now. I hope I didn't overwhelm her.

"I didn't know why," she continues after a moment. "I thought I'd done something wrong. But I couldn't think of anything. And I didn't want to just show up at your house because I was afraid I'd upset you even more. Then I saw Rose and realized. The way I felt. About you. It didn't look like romcoms. It didn't fit our plan. We didn't meet at a beach or a party. Eyes locking and . . ." She's rambling a little bit, but I understand her, like she's always understood me, and I think I know what she's about to say. "Rose is cool. But they aren't you."

We sit in silence for a moment, absorbing each other's words. A fly flits around one of the cupcakes and I wave it away.

"You got my favorite," Talia says in a soft voice.

"Of course."

Her eyes move up and meet mine.

"I'm really sorry," I say again.

"Thank you," she whispers.

"What can I do?" I ask. "I mean, if you need a break from us . . ." I swallow.

She shakes her head. "No, no. I don't want any more breaks." She picks up her cupcake. "Can I eat this?"

I smile. "Definitely."

I pick mine up and we each take a bite, chewing in silence. The taste of the chocolate frosting helps ground me. Talia eats with one hand, her other hand petting the soft fleece of the blanket. That's exactly why I picked it—I know how much she loves soft textures.

When she finishes her cupcake, she looks back at me.

"Talia," I say. Her mouth curves in the tiniest way, more hope than smile. "I know I messed up and I'm not perfect, but I'm going to do everything I can not to do that again. If you only want to be friends, that's OK. But . . . I want you to be my girl-friend. If you want to."

Her eyes fill with tears again, and my heart seizes, but then she speaks. "I'd like that. I . . . I love you, too. As a friend. And in the romantic way."

"I love *you*," I say, voice cracking.

We both laugh, wiping our faces, relief and amazement flooding my body.

"Can I hold your hand?" she asks.

"Of course."

We each get up on our knees and scoot toward each other until we're face to face. This is the closest I've been to Talia in weeks and my heart's pounding. We sit back down, crossed knees touching, and take each other's hands.

"I totally get why you were freaked out," she says. "I was, too."

"Thank you," I say.

Then we look at each other—really *look* at each other—eyes traveling over each other's faces. I let myself linger on everything I never did before: the perfect thick arches of her brows; her skin, tanned and freckled from the sun; the strong bridge of her nose; the dimple in the center of her chin.

And her lips. Thin, with the tiniest, sweetest cupid's bow, the bottom lip slightly bigger than the top. Usually, they turn up a little at the corners, but right now they're totally relaxed, the way they do when Talia isn't masking. The sight almost makes me cry again. She's comfortable with me, like I am with her. Even after everything.

"Can I . . ." I bring my gaze up to hers, and she's already looking at me. "Can I kiss you?"

She nods, a huge smile breaking out across her face. We take a deep breath at the same time—then explode in nervous giggles.

"You lean in first," she says.

I nod and lean forward, and so does she, but we come in too fast, and—

"Ow!" We both pull back, rubbing our teeth where they clunked together.

She laughs. "One more time?"

I shake myself out and then clasp her hands. She squeezes once. I lean forward, slowly, and so does she, and then *it's happening.*

We're kissing.

Her lips are soft, and she tastes like coffee and chocolate, the flavor of her cupcake. Our mouths open and holy wow, our lips fit together and the kiss blends into another one. *I'm kissing Talia. I'm kissing Talia! And it's awesome.*

She pulls back and we're both grinning like clowns, staring at each other. Her cheeks are flushed, and mine are warm, too.

She clears her throat. "Whoa."

I nod.

"That was my first kiss," she says.

"Mine too!" I screech, and she bursts out laughing, squeezing my hands.

"Do you want some LaCroix?" she asks.

"Yes. Yeah." My brain is still scrambled from that kiss. My first kiss. My totally life-changing first kiss with *Talia.*

She hands me one, and we crack them open together. We each take a big gulp and stare at each other, then break into giggles again. My cheeks hurt from smiling.

"Obviously I have no frame of reference, but you're a really good kisser," she says. It's the most Talia thing she could say, and it's my turn to laugh, shaking my head. She eyes me. "What?"

"Nothing. This is just awesome," I say, pressing my hands to my face with a huge grin. "You're a really good kisser, too. As far as I know."

"Oh." She covers her mouth. "I did not realize how that sounded."

"No, no, I love it," I say. "It's so you. And I love you. As a friend. And romantically."

She nods, blushing harder. "Good."

I raise my can. "A toast. To us."

"To us." She says, and we clink them together. I take a drink, and the carbonation sparkles all the way down to my stomach.

Talia's my girlfriend. I'm Talia's girlfriend.

"Can I kiss you again?" I ask.

"Absolutely," she says, and we both lean forward.

CHAPTER TWENTY-FOUR

I WAKE UP BEFORE my alarm the next morning and sit up, breathing in the fresh summer air drifting through my open window. My phone chirps, and I reach for it to see a text from Talia: Have a great time at practice today!

I grin at the screen and text back a line of smiling emojis with hearts dancing around their heads. It's fitting that it's the first emoji to pop up when I type the phrase "in love" into the text box.

The group chat lights up. Kev wants us all to meet at World Pizza later. I thumbs-up the suggestion and toss my phone into my bag, along with my basketball shoes and a water bottle. A pair of shorts and a tank top from the floor pass the sniff test, and then I'm thumping down the stairs to grab some breakfast before I head out.

Ella's already there, gulping down cereal before she heads out, too. "You look all . . ." She waves a hand at me. "Sparkly."

"Hayley and Talia are dating!" I turn and see Sam grinning at us. "They made up yesterday and kissed and everything!"

"Sam!" I shriek. "It's *my* news!"

"Sorry," they say, shrugging, in a tone that suggests they are very much not sorry at all. "I overheard you telling Mom and Dad about it when you got home."

I grab a handful of blueberry snack bars from the cabinet, glaring at them. "You mean you were eavesdropping. *Again.*"

They shrug, grinning.

I roll my eyes. "Whatever. Yes, we're dating," I say.

Ella slow claps. "*Finally.*"

"Ugh!" I stuff the snacks into my bag. "You two are so annoying." I rush past them toward the door.

"We love you," Sam calls after me.

"Love you, too," I shout, waving my hand above my head, and then I'm out the door.

I have plenty of time before the bus to get my headphones on and eat a snack bar, savoring each bite while Janelle Monáe pumps me up. My whole body is fizzing like the LaCroix I drank last night. I feel like I'm flying, like the world is sharper and more beautiful than I've ever seen it. When the bus comes rattling down the street, it looks like a chariot, here to take me into the next chapter of my life. My life with a girlfriend. My life, more importantly, with *Talia* as my girlfriend.

I'm right on time to practice, jogging up as Jaya unlocks the gym door for the team.

Sherika holds up her hand for a high five. "You look wide awake."

I meet her hand with mine for a satisfying smack. It feels like

Sherika's become a friend over the course of the summer, and I love that for us. I've never befriended a former crush before. "I'm ready to dunk on y'all."

Jaya snorts, and for a minute I think I've gotten on her nerves, but then she swings the door open. "All right, sophomore, show me what you got."

"I'm a *junior*, excuse you," I say as I dart past.

They cackle behind me, our shoes squeaking on the gym floor. On the sideline, I change out of my sandals and into my socks and sneakers as they unlock the gear room and wheel out the bin of basketballs. Sherika tosses one to me and I turn, square up, and jump. The ball leaves my hands and arcs through the air, passing through the basket with a clean swish. A perfect three-pointer. Jaya whistles and Sherika whoops.

I pass the ball to Sherika. "It'll be good to have you on varsity this year," she says.

"What?" I laugh.

She shrugs. "You heard me. You better bring your A game to tryouts in September."

"Challenge accepted," I say. We smile at each other, and then she turns and sinks a three-pointer of her own.

My teammates trickle in, and maybe it's just the girlfriend high I'm riding, but the vibes are immaculate. I get a couple fist-bumps and nods, no one gives me the side eye, and Sherika puts Beyoncé's new album on.

"Morning," Mariah says as she steps up beside me at the free-throw line. We shoot at the same time and her ball makes the basket, knocking mine away. "Got 'em!" she crows as I race after my ball.

"Guess what?" I say when I get back.

"What?"

I smirk. "Guess."

She eyes me. "OK, what's different . . . you're peppy as fuck, for one." She scans me. "You look like you're about to vibrate out your skin—and you're grinning like a fool." Her eyes go wide. "Oh my god. Your bestie."

"Talia's my girlfriend!" I screech.

She screams, and the whole gym goes silent.

We look around. Everyone is frozen in place, staring at us, and then one of the seniors starts laughing and clapping. One by one, all the players join in, even a few players who are just coming in and don't seem to understand why we're clapping but do it anyway.

I take a bow, and the clapping dies down as people go back to their warm-ups.

Mariah high-fives me. "That's my girl."

I grin. "I'm back in the game, baby."

As I walk up to Talia's house that afternoon, my stomach starts flipping out again. It's not exactly anxiety, but it's not the same fizzing from this morning. This is the first time I'm seeing Talia in person since last night, and even though we texted back and forth all day, part of me feels like this isn't quite real. *Do I kiss her when I see her? Hug her? How do girlfriends greet each other usually? How will Talia and I decide to greet each other?*

The door opens as I come up the front walk, and I stop short, a smile taking over my whole face. Talia stands there with a smile to match mine.

She lifts a hand, biting her lower lip. "Hi."

I wave back. "Hey."

We stand there, just grinning at each other.

"So, um . . . do you wanna come in?" she asks, and I nod vigorously.

I follow her upstairs and scan her room while she shuffles through the papers on her desk, looking for her phone. It's the first time I've been in here since before we started dating. *When was the last time I was here?* My eyes land on a watermelon-print blouse of hers hanging over the edge of her laundry basket.

Oh wow. The last time I was here was the day of her first date with Rose. The day I helped her pick out her outfit and she made that comment about me being in her bed, and—

The butterflies are flapping wildly inside my chest. Her bed's right there. It's neatly made, the purple comforter smoothed out, the pillows in their lavender and cream and galaxy-pattern pillowcases all plumped up and sitting against the headboard. Her stuffed elephant sits in the center.

"Hayley?" I look over. Talia's standing there holding her phone, looking at me with a frown. "You OK?"

"Totally." I nod quickly. "Just spacing out." *Thinking about her bed and lying on it and—and I'm not going to tell her that. We aren't there yet. I'm not there.*

She smiles. "I almost forgot something."

"What?"

"I wanted to kiss you hello."

"Oh!"

"You're blushing," she says. I put my hands to my cheeks. They're definitely warm.

"It's a sunburn," I say. "A special kind. It only appears when my girlfriend says cute things to me."

She laughs. "You're adorable."

We stare at each other and step closer at the same time, her hands going to my face, mine on her waist—and then her lips are on mine. It's easier every time we kiss. I feel like I'm getting the hang of it now, and our mouths fit together perfectly. My arms move to pull her closer.

We kiss for a long time, until my head goes fuzzy, and then she steps back. Her face is flushed all the way down her neck, her eyes sparkling. I wonder if I look the same way.

"That was." I clear my throat. "Good. Yeah."

She nods. "Agreed. Very good. We should do that again. You know. For science."

"Mm-hmm." I nod and reach for her.

We kiss again, and my body is more than fizzing; it's all shooting stars and comets, lost in the universe of her. The skin of her bare upper arms, the back of her neck, her face as I cup it with both my hands, is all so unbelievably soft. She sighs into my mouth, and it's the most beautiful sound I've ever heard.

She startles, pulling back.

"What's up?" I ask through my kiss-drunk haze.

"Sorry. Your phone dinged. It startled me." She grins. "You didn't hear it?"

"Not at all." I giggle and pull my phone out of my pocket, then hold it up to show her the message from Kevin in the group chat: HURRY UP WE'RE HUNGRYYYYYYY!!!!!!

"We better get going," she says. She reaches out a hand, and I reach out mine, and then we're holding hands.

Just like that.

We're really here. We're really dating.

"Shall we?" she asks, cheeks pink.

We stay hand in hand all the way out of the house and down her front stairs. I can't stop thinking about kissing her and how much I want to do it again. When I first realized my crush, I was so worried about us maybe breaking up some day that I never stopped to think how amazing things could be. But now, with our fingers entwined, my fear is a distant echo. I know that no matter what happens, no matter how hard things get, our friendship can survive it.

The afternoon is humid, and after a while my hand is sweaty in her grasp. She squeezes once and lets go.

"Too . . ." She wiggles her fingers and I laugh. We both wipe our palms on our clothes and smile at each other.

"I never thought about what it would be like to hold hands in the summer," I say.

She furrows her brow, thinking for a second. "What about this?" she asks and then links her pinky through mine.

Instant butterflies. "That's good."

We walk like that the whole rest of the way, sometimes talking, sometimes quiet, sometimes looking at the people and buildings and cars as they pass, sometimes looking at each other. We giggle a lot, and it's hard to keep eye contact for long because all I can think about is how cute she is.

Our friends are already there in the back booth when we arrive. They look up guiltily from their half-eaten slices.

"We couldn't wait," Kev says.

"I was getting hangry," Jacob says.

"It's not good when he's hangry," Bri adds.

Karina takes another bite, waving at us.

I snort and shake my head. "It's fine." I turn to Talia. "What do you want?"

"I can get my own," she says.

"It's OK. I want to," I say.

She smiles. "The cheese with peach slices on it?" She stims, lifting her shoulders up and down, and it's the cutest thing I've ever seen.

I bite my lower lip. "You got it."

"*Oh my god.*" We look back at them and Jacob is staring at us, hands clasped together, eyes gleaming. "You're dating!"

"You knew that," I say. Last night, after me and Talia's picnic, they all came back to meet us, and for a full five minutes we all screamed in excitement about it until we jumped in the water to celebrate.

"Still." He waves a hand. "Just watching you—you're ordering for her! You're holding pinkies. I can't even."

Kev grins. "We're really happy for you."

I glance at Bri, and they just smile at me.

Karina kisses them on the cheek. "I guess we're not the cutest couple in the group anymore," she says.

"Whatever!" Talia waves a hand. "You were the only couple before."

"And now we have competition." Karina puts her fists up.

"Pizza first." I point at her. "Fighting later."

She puts up her hands, granting a truce, and I make my way up to the counter. As I wait for our slices to warm, I watch the group shuffle to make room for us. Jacob pulls over one of the extra chairs to sit at the end, and Kev slides to the inside of the booth so Talia can sit. There's an open space on her other side.

For me.

We all hang out there until it's late. There's a small rush of people from the end of a sports game at one of the stadiums downtown, but I hardly notice the noise. I'm too focused on my friends' glowing faces, the warmth and weight of Talia's hand on my leg, watching her eat pizza beside me. After a while, the shop empties out again, and one of the cooks swings by to let us know they're starting to close down.

We finish the last of our slices, dump our dishes in the bin, and wander out into the night. We decide to go back to Kev's house to hang out, so we cut over to Jackson Street for the walk up to the Central District. As we walk, the group unbunches and forms pairs: Bri and Karina leading the way, Kev and Jacob chattering about a new video game they're both excited about, and me and Talia bringing up the rear.

"I have a question for you," she says. I tilt my head. "You know the summer love strategy?"

"I'm not sure . . ." I put a hand up to my chin and make a serious face. "Can you remind me?"

She swats my shoulder lightly and I dodge away, giggling. We come back together, pinkies linking as we pass under the streetlight behind our friends.

"I was thinking," she says. "We should do it over again, but this time as dates. I know there aren't any concerts or parties coming up, but . . . do you want to go swimming with me tomorrow? I heard a lot of queer people swim at Madison Park Beach over here."

I look over at her, my chest swelling like I'm about to float off the ground and away into the stars. "Talia. That's so sweet."

"Well." She shrugs and ducks her head. "I just . . . I really liked the strategy because it was something we were doing together, and I want to do it again, but this time the way it should have been: as our romantic summer dates."

My eyes are stinging now, and I stop, pulling her to me. We hold each other tight in the darkness under the overpass. "I would love to."

"Hey!" We look up ahead. In the glow of the streetlight, our friends are waving. "Get a room!"

"*You* get a room!" I yell back.

"Well, we'd be in mine already if you weren't stopping to make out every ten seconds!" Kev shouts.

"We are not!" Talia calls as we race up toward them.

Our friends turn and we chase them all the way up the street, laughing until none of us can breathe and we have to slow down. I'm sweating, and my legs are burning, but I'm OK with that.

Talia's pinky slips around mine as we all stand panting at the crosswalk, waiting for the light to turn, and when I look at her, she's smiling at me. I get that fizzing, sparkling, shooting star feeling again, but I'm not out in space this time. I'm standing on the ground, basking in the glow. *So this is what it feels like when the person you have a crush on likes you back.*

I'm so glad it's Talia.

Ray Stoeve is the author of the young adult novel *Between Perfect and Real*, which received a starred review and was a 2021 Junior Library Guild Gold Standard selection, and *Arden Grey*. They also contributed to the young adult anthology *Take the Mic: Fictional Stories of Everyday Resistance*. They received a 2016–2017 Made at Hugo House Fellowship and created the YA/MG Trans and Nonbinary Voices Masterlist, a database that tracks all books in those age categories written by trans authors about trans characters. When they're not writing, they can be found gardening, making art in other mediums, or hiking their beloved Pacific Northwest.